FORTUNE'S DAUGHTER

FORTUNE'S DAUGHTER

Elizabeth Lord

This first world edition published in Great Britain 2002 by
SEVERN HOUSE PUBLISHERS LTD of
9–15 High Street, Sutton, Surrey SM1 1DF.
This first world edition published in the USA 2002 by
SEVERN HOUSE PUBLISHERS INC of
595 Madison Avenue, New York, N.Y. 10022.

Nottinghamshire County Council
Community Services

Askews

£18.99

British Library Cataloguing in Publication Data

Lord, Elizabeth
    Fortune's Daughter
    1. Cromwell, Oliver - Family
    2. Great Britain - History - Commonwealth and Protectorate,
        1649-1660 - Fiction
    3. Historical fiction
    I. Title
    823.9'14 [F]

ISBN 0-7278-5873-4

Typeset by Palimpsest Book Production Ltd.,
Polmont, Stirlingshire, Scotland.
Printed and bound in Great Britain by
MPG Books Ltd., Bodmin, Cornwall.

One

1655

A t her window, Frances Cromwell – now a princess – sat gazing out over the lawns and woods of Hampton Court Palace.

Her mind was far away, thinking back to that day, several weeks ago now, when her father – Oliver Cromwell, the Lord Protector of England – had wed the man she loved to another, right there in front of her eyes, and she having to stand helplessly by while the cruel deed was done. It had been the worst day of her young life, a day she would never forget, even if she lived to be eighty.

Before that, life had been so sweet, so perfect, and would have been even more perfect if her father had finally seen her point of view and wed her to the chaplain, Jeremiah White. How could she have imagined it would all end in such a way? She still hadn't quite recovered from the cruelty of it, and wondered if she ever would, despite the smiles she presented to all those at court.

A fortnight she had lain in her bed, too uncaring of the world to stir, while the whole family grew increasingly alarmed. Until it had finally dawned on everyone that she hadn't been ill but merely overcome by all that had happened. But what young girl wouldn't

1

feel that way, knowing herself in love only to have that love snatched from her by her own father and in such a cruel manner?

After the couple – wed by her father's orders there on the spot – had left her room, where the marriage had been performed, she'd fainted right away, alone. She had regained consciousness to find herself in bed, a sea of worried faces floating above her and Doctor Goddard, her father's own physician, bending over her.

Her father, she discovered later, had spent hours on his knees praying for her recovery. But with a heart so hardened against him, she had merely thought that well he might pray after the way he had served her.

It was mainly her sister, Mary, who brought news to her, sitting beside her, pummelling her mattress and pillows to make them more comfortable and talking as though she were in normal health and spirits. Frances learned that their father had become so ill-tempered that none dared approach him, and that time after time he had gone into such fits of rage that one Royalist pamphlet reported him to have fallen dead from an uncontrollable distemper.

Parliament assumed these outbursts to stem from political disasters of late – a revolt of settlers in Barbados against the English government, a humiliating withdrawal from Hispaniola, superior English forces put to shameful flight by a handful of Spanish, through poorly planned strategy and lack of liaison, over a thousand men lost from wounds, disease and lack of food, Colonel Venables and Admiral Penn each accusing the other of hogging rations as supplies dwindled. Both had raced home to complain to His Highness about the other, only to come up against his uncontrollable rage and be thrown into the Tower for incompetence.

Royalists, Fifth Monarchists and unfriendly nations had made much of these raging fits, but only Frances knew the underlying truth – he was feeling an uneasy guilt for having been instrumental in causing her 'illness' – as she preferred to call it – through his handling of the business of her and his chaplain, Jeremiah White.

Whenever Papa came into her room, she hadn't missed the sadness in his eyes even though she turned her face from him. But bitterness against him couldn't last forever. He was her father.

And indeed the bitterness did slowly start to fade, even if her sense of loss didn't. Had Jerry hurled defiance at her father in those last minutes, might he have consented to the marriage? She would never know. But as Mary pointed out, Jeremiah White had been tested and had been found false, a coward.

As Mary leaned forward and hugged her for eventually sitting up, contempt for the man began slowly to fill the empty place his betrayal had left. Although it hurt whenever she thought of it, she must put it from her. Again Mary was right – he wasn't worth it, and all this pining wouldn't bring him back. Taking a deep breath, she sat straighter. It did some good.

An hour later she was up. Her new maid, Marie, was summoned to dress her and comb her tangled curls into soft ringlets. Her former maid, Margaret, was gone – she was now the wife of Jeremiah White and would keep his apartments and carry out her mundane wifely duties and not be seen again, but just as well.

Mary had asked, 'Do you not wonder that he might

have been slyly meeting her between times of meeting you and she the informer that day?' Frances had instantly dismissed the remark, though it did put a thought into her mind – that she would never know the answer. But she did wonder if he was happy in his married state. He never looked so when she glimpsed him from time to time at Hampton Court. He made a pretence of not seeing her, and though it reopened the wound to bleed a flux of the old yearning, she took some comfort in the thought that his had been a great fall from what he'd apparently hoped for, and it helped strengthen her resolve to put him from her. But it was hard.

'Lately I had rather expected the subject of William Dutton to arise again.'

She had told Mary some time ago of the will and her father's promise, and at the time Mary had seethed with indignation for her.

'You must prevail against it with all your might,' she had advised, but Frances had already done so by then. Though lately some of her spirit had left her, despite a resolve to stand proud.

'I no longer care who I marry,' she sighed now. 'William Dutton is as good as any, I suppose.' Yet though his name did crop up occasionally, Papa never mentioned marriage again.

Her brother Richard, on one of his rare visits to Whitehall, spoke of it in passing, but only to caution her against hurrying too early into marriage.

'Barely seventeen,' he said as they stood on the steps leading down to the river with its smooth tide throwing glints of summer sunshine back into their eyes. 'Plenty of time yet. My sweet Dorothy was well twenty-two when we wed. You are nowhere near ready, little sister,' he teased with a rich laugh. 'Do I err in looking upon you as such still? I swear there are times you look older than I, so deep has your expression become. Nevertheless, do linger awhile in that happy state of innocence that's with us for so short a time.'

France gave a secret, sad smile. He had no idea, being so taken up with his own life, that her happy state of innocence had gone with Jeremiah White and would never return.

As the summer of 1655 progressed, the name of William Dutton faded before another name, far more splendid on the family's lips.

'George Villiers,' announced Mary, always first to come by any news, like a diligent housemaid raking out the minutest cinder from beneath a fire basket. 'George Villiers, Duke of Buckingham.' There was a hint of envy in her tone. 'They make him out to be the handsomest of men. He has been making enquiries in your direction, and Papa does not appear opposed to it. Though why such haste to see you wed I cannot understand. I am older than you.'

But of course Mary knew. Older she might be, but it was the youngest daughter who was the problem, while Mary had never given Papa a moment's worry. The quicker Papa saw his youngest daughter safely settled, the easier he would feel.

'You don't seem over-pleased,' remarked Mary.

'I am pleased enough.' It seemed that Mary assumed she had by now got over Jeremiah White. None could ever know another's pain unless they had suffered it themselves.

'*Pleased enough!*' Mary glared at her. 'I'd be over-joyed were it I. How much more can you want? The Duke of Buckingham – you'll be a duchess.'

Frances shook her head. 'I rather doubt it will ever take place. The first Duke of Buckingham, George Villiers' father, gained his title and lands from King James and was a great favourite of the Stuarts. Father confiscated those estates, so why should George Villiers look to wed the daughter of his enemy except to regain his lands? But Papa's no fool and must see through his request.'

Mary turned sharply from her to gaze out of the window at the vast parklands of Hampton Court, whose trees were beginning to be touched by autumn tints.

'Come and look,' she said, and as Frances came to join her and they linked arms, she went on, 'You should look beyond your nose, Frankie. This is ours, given to Papa by a grateful and loving nation. But George Villiers is no fool – I am certain he has some secret alliance with Papa regarding Charles Stuart and those who support him.' Her grip on Frances' arm tightened. 'You estimate that by marriage to one of the Protector's daughters, his father will be returned his estates? But don't you see? At the same time, as a close friend of Charles Stuart, George Villiers marrying you would reconcile the Royalists and bring harmony to the country. They'd never rise up against us were we united with such a close associate of Charles Stuart.'

'And I am merely a pawn in their political games?' hissed Frances, making an effort to pull away from the sisterly embrace.

Mary gave her a look of exasperation. 'Were it me, I'd not simper at such an opportunity.'

'Simper?'

'Pretending you are not worthy of your station. I never see you protest when gentlemen bow to *Princess Frances*! For my part I find it most pleasing to be addressed as Princess Mary and I've no qualms in saying so.'

Releasing herself from Mary, Frances swung away from the window. 'We've become far too high and mighty. It frightens me how rapid has been our ascent, as though we've clambered to the top of a high rock that one day may tumble down into a dark valley, bearing us with it.'

'How very poetic,' scoffed Mary. 'Were he still our tutor, Andrew Marvell would applaud you! You remind me so of Mama, ever crying after simplicity. If she had her way she would never dine in the Banqueting Hall or here in the great hall. She would rather eat country fare, black puddings and stews in the kitchen. Why, she still makes her own buttermilk from the cows she keeps for her use in St James's Park. It is so embarrassing.'

'All people of standing have their own dairy herds,' defended Frances.

'But not in St James's Park, like some peasant. People of good standing keep their herds on their own farms. But Mama must have her three or four by her and must make her own buttermilk rather than get servants to do it. And I swear she is more at home with her sewing circles for daughters of humble London ministers than mingling with those who throng Papa's court. People call her Queen Joan, sometimes the Kitchen Queen, and even Protectoress Parsimony. There are tales that she even weighs out food for banquets, as soldiers weigh out rations before a battle.'

'How can you repeat such evil lies!' cried Frances. 'It is our mother you are speaking of, Mall. Our guests ever congratulate her on her splendid dinners.'

Mary smirked. 'It is our master chefs who prepare them these days.'

'But still under her direction, and she has never stinted anyone.'

'I am only saying what is being said abroad. I know they're evil lies. But it is she who prompts them, with her country manners and her shyness of public life.'

'And I would have her no other way,' concluded Frances angrily. 'How can you be so lenient towards those who lampoon our mother so?'

Frances had made a special point of tackling her father on this subject, saying, 'They should be thrown into the Tower!'

His reply had been a dry burst of laughter. 'Were I to throw everyone who makes fun of us in the Tower, there'd not be enough room for all to lie down.'

'But she heeds them, personally.'

'Then she should not. And you too must learn that those raised to great height must expect some amount of low wit from the envious. I do not hold this country to tyranny, Frankie – the people are free to speak their opinion so long as it does not provoke active aggression. So peace, my dear.'

'But I hate to see Mama so—'

He had hushed her with a finger to his lips, his grey eyes twinkling. 'If I care not a hat feather for low jests, neither should she. But I will comfort her if that pleases you. Now away – I have my duties to attend to first.'

Elizabeth Cromwell was in her chamber with Madame

Duret and two maidservants, sorting linen to send to the poor of St Martin-in-the-Fields. Dismissing them, Oliver seated himself down on an oak settle.

'I've come to ask your advice, my dear Joan,' he began affectionately. 'Do you think it wise for me to negotiate any further with the Duke of Buckingham on possible marriage to one or other of our daughters, say, Frances?'

He waited, but seeing she was not inclined to reply yet, went on. 'The Royalist uprising earlier this year has worried me greatly, for all it was swiftly put down.' He heaved a deep sigh. 'There are times, my dear, when I feel the reins of office slipping.'

Now she came to life, defending him. 'Oh, no, dear, they never will.'

Heartened by her words, he brightened. 'An alliance with George Villiers through a marriage contract would alleviate certain discontents. The return of his estates could easily be given in exchange for infiltration into Royalist plots and Charles Stuart's own plans, of which Villiers has much knowledge.'

Weighted against it would be the reaction of the Parliamentarians, some still recalling the days of the Good Old Cause, blind to the fact that times, by their very nature, must change. But this had nothing to do with his wife, had nothing to do with what he had come to discuss with her. He changed tack, patting the settle for her to sit beside him. He took her hand as she did so.

'I'm informed that certain vulgar jests directed at your person have caused you distress, my dear.'

She gazed down at the linen and clothing that had been piled on the floor. 'There is no need to concern yourself with a silly woman's notions. Perhaps I'd not be so hurt by them were you here more often. Your duties take you from me for such long hours.'

He pushed away some fripperies on the floor near him with his foot in a gesture of irritation. 'God knows, I do try to find time to be with you.'

'Which seems less and less. My life is but half a life when you are not here. Could we be as companionable as once we were before we became so high, I might not find those jests so hurtful.'

'Were we to be as we once were,' he said, 'there'd be no cause for mean jests from mean little men who'd now see us brought down because they have not the wit to bring themselves up.'

'Perhaps it is us who are found wanting,' she said quietly.

Refusing to look at him, she played with the hem of a discarded garment of blue wool. 'Were we to conduct ourselves with more humility, much of the cruel jesting would cease. Your court becomes ever more like that of a king. Crowds seeking to gain favours from you, some even pestering me. Ladies show off their finery and men strut like peacocks. We no longer seem to fulfil our tasks with love of the Lord but—'

'Do you say I lack humility?'

There was a hardness in his tone, and she looked up to see his sparse eyebrows arched. He didn't wait for her reply. 'God entrusted me with this great country and has been with me in all things connected with it. Ever and again I have gone on my knees imploring to be released of this burden but am guided ever on. I am not responsible for men who look to put me up high, who look to show me their respect. Were we to become as once we were, Joan, that respect would be blown away like a feather on the wind and with it this country's greatness which by God's grace I have built.' Having rid himself of ill humour he chuckled, suddenly playful. 'Would you have the head of this nation be re-employed mending shoes for other men's feet?' She did not smile. 'Our Lord washed the feet of his own disciples. Was that a thing to be mocked?' His roar of anger made her flinch. 'This is intolerable, Elizabeth! You use the Lord's name for your petty argument? I came to offer you words of comfort, and you abuse it as you abuse His name.' He leapt up from the settle. 'So you to your duties and leave me to mine.'

She too stood up. 'And what of your duties? Do they include playing the gallant to certain fair ladies?'

'You lose me, Elizabeth.' He glowered at her but she would not be cowed.

'All London buzzes over how you dance attendance upon Countess Dysart and, more recently, Frances Lambert, as though she were the light of your heart. Am I grown so plain that—'

'Enough, Elizabeth!' He strode for the door, but paused to look at her. 'You were never plain. I still see in you the sweet, rounded maid I married. But you will make yourself so by ugly jealousies, having nothing else to occupy your mind. My friendship with Frances Lambert is above suspicion and I will not be rebuked for it.'

'Then why,' she shot at him, 'is it jested all around London that His Highness's Instrument of Government is to be found under Lady Lambert's petticoats? And some go so far as to merely call it His Highness's

11

Instrument! Whether such be true or not, it shows that the Head of State lets himself be brought down to such disadvantage like . . . like a debauched king besotted by his mistress.'

'Silence, Elizabeth! This is unseemly.'

'No, I will have my say. You are not a king but a respected and God-fearing leader of this country. How can you let yourself be so mocked? It hurts me beyond measure.'

'There is no more to my engaging in spiritual and virtuous meditation with Frances Lambert than in my brotherly affection for her husband. As for the Countess Dysart, I grant she is a woman of fine looks, character and charm enough to turn any man's head, with a quick wit and a clever mind, but she is over-witty and over-clever, and with too many Royalist connections. So rest easy on both scores, my wife, and listen not to mischief-makers lest they disturb the blessed tranquillity of our pleasant marriage which, if it happens, will be your doing, Elizabeth, not mine.'

He was halfway along the corridor before he realised that in his anger he hadn't gone fully into the matter of George Villiers, and hadn't received an answer to the question he'd gone to Elizabeth about. He could hardly return now. He would speak of it another time, when he was calmer.

Meanwhile, an hour or two with the Lamberts would put him in a better frame of mind. An evening's indulgence with good wine and good conversation with the attractive Frances – and John Lambert, should he be there – would soon soothe bruised spirits. On this thought Oliver lengthened his stride.

*　　*　　*

George Villiers had weighed the wisdom of getting his lands back by an alliance with the dubious usurper against their more legitimate return on the restoration of Charles Stuart at some later date – which he was sure would come about – and had finally decided on the latter course.

His Highness was furious. Condemning Buckingham out of hand, he immediately began to cast about for another suitor for his wilful youngest daughter.

Frances was furious. 'I feel I am being auctioned off at a cattle market,' she raged to her mother. 'So few seem eager to claim me, I'm sure I am grown plain. It's degrading being offered first to this one then to that.'

Elizabeth took her hand. She wasn't one to be demonstrative, but Frances looking so woebegone warranted that reassuring touch.

'Your father thinks only of your good. Give him a little time and he will negotiate a much finer marriage for you. There are many to choose from.'

'And be spurned by.'

'Who could spurn you, my dear? Villiers' response was political. I think he saw you as positively charming.'

'There are many who've already spurned me – I've been passed over by one who evidently favoured a mere servant above me. And William Dutton apparently never protested at no longer being considered. Now Buckingham waves me aside.'

Her mother smiled indulgently. 'Oh, come! It was you who spurned young Master Dutton. And the Duke of Buckingham was but a passing thought of your father's, of little consequence, nothing more. Wait and

13

see, Frankie – your father will contract you a marriage that will delight your heart when it comes.'

Frances was no longer sure her heart would ever be delighted again. She confided that sentiment to her brother Richard a few days later when he decided to grace Whitehall with his presence for a while to enjoy those fine apartments given to him after the Admiralty Commission had been expelled.

'I resent being used for political bargaining,' she told him.

It was Saturday afternoon – one of those golden October afternoons warm enough to sit out on the parapet that divided the Thames from the gardens. Behind them was the red brick of the Tudor palace, its intricate maze of buildings dwarfed by the high, square bulk of the Banqueting Hall that glowed yellow under the sun's slanting, orange rays. Even the river running smooth on a strong tide was like a river of gold, the busy traffic that plied up and down it black against the dazzle. A golden afternoon indeed, with the calm that often comes before a wild winter.

Richard had been sitting with Dorothy when she had decided to join them, but Doll left soon after with little Beth's nurse, who came to fetch her over something the child had done.

Frances and Dick remained sitting to appreciate the calm of the river traffic, and little by little Frances told him of Jerry White and the effect it was still having on her, finding in him a receptive ear. It was easy to talk to him about it all. He too was a rebel, though quietly so, a kindred spirit who had managed to escape the Puritan net of family rules as they had been relaxed with the passing of years. She told it simply

14

and he listened, not interrupting until finally her voice died away.

'You still love him,' he said at last.

'I am embittered by his conduct. And ashamed.'

'That's no answer.' He laid a slim hand on hers. 'Embittered or ashamed, love may be renewed by the slightest glance.'

'But he is married now.'

'Would your heart not melt anew should he beg your forgiveness, be he married or not?'

'No,' she stated firmly, surprising herself. 'My pride would not let it.'

Dick's handsome face split with a grin. 'That is a more convincing answer. It is natural to fall in love and primness has no place, nor does shame, if love is honest and selfless. That you fell in love unwisely has my sympathy, but your being unashamed by it would cause me great pride in you, my sweet sister. So away with feelings of shame! And do not put yourself down thinking no one will have you in marriage. You are pretty enough for a king. And soon there'll be someone who will turn his eyes on you and make your heart beat so fast you'll hardly be able to breathe and will forget all else.' The hand on hers tightened a fraction. 'Until that day, heed my words, Frankie. Don't let yourself be the object of any political negotiations through marriage, no matter who is put out by it. It's your happiness they dally with.'

She gave him a reproachful glance. 'It's all very well for you. You and Henry married your own choice. Even had Papa disapproved, as men, you'd both still have married as you wished. A woman cannot ride so roughshod. No one understands how I feel. Everyone except Mary is happily married, and she thinks only of a wealthy and titled husband. She has never been in love to know how I feel. As for Papa, he has no feelings for me other than to get me off his hands as quickly as he can.'

'You're wrong, Frankie. He cares a great deal for your happiness.'

'You see?' she exclaimed. 'Even *you* don't understand. I wish I'd never told you—'

She broke off when she saw Dorothy coming towards them, her gait cumbersome. Dorothy was heavily pregnant, the child expected around Christmas. Seeing her so burdened, Frances forgot about her own problems and hoped that this one would survive beyond infancy. Her last, born just after the death of little Mary in September 1654, had hardly seen the year out before joining her sister in May this year. Strange, thought Frances as she left the two together, Dick had fathered all daughters, as though his nature was too gentle to beget sons. And Papa so longed for a grandson.

Dear Richard, she was sorry to have rebuked him just now, though she was sure he would bear her no grudge, for it wasn't in his nature to bear grudges.

Two

W hen Dick visited Hampton Court a fortnight later, he brought with him a group of young people Frances' own age, full of pranks and jests. Among them was George Poulter, the lively Henry Baxter, and Robert Rich, grandson of the Earl of Warwick, a good Puritan, for all his peerage.

It was a pity that she was introduced to them all only that one time, for from then on, not only did bad weather keep the family away from their weekend residence, but also Mama fell prey to a stomach upset that lasted almost until Christmas.

Frances' sister Betty too had such stomach pains that her father ordered her to move into Whitehall, where Doctor Goddard could keep an eye on her, for she had become so thin that he feared for her.

Whether it was anxiety for his wife and daughter or merely pressure from work, Oliver began again to suffer from the painful stone that had laid him low in Scotland. Goddard prescribed long, bumpy coach rides and arduous gallops to help break up the stone, and they did seem to help.

'At least,' offered Mary as they sat through a doleful Christmas period with the reek of physic and potions all around, 'we've Betty's children to gladden his heart

17

and keep us occupied. Little Henry and little Cromwell are such handsome boys and little Martha is as dear to Papa's heart as any child could be. He shows her off to every foreign visitor and takes delight in their admiration of her.'

'These apartments bulge with children,' said Frances, nibbling discontentedly at a sweetmeat. She'd been so buoyed up by those young people Richard had introduced, especially the fine-looking Robert Rich, that she felt even more restricted here because of it – all this illness around her and the bevy of fractious children that had come to stay.

Mama had insisted Dorothy have her baby at Whitehall – it turned out to be yet another girl, to whom Doll had given her own name. Born a week ago, it was another puny little thing, but it had wriggled into the world so easily that in a week Doll was as chirpy as a cricket.

'Her babies may be puny,' remarked Mary after admiring the tiny scrap, 'but she seems able to bring them forth as readily as a rabbit its kits! And this one's equally sweet.'

'A pity the same cannot be said of Bridget's brood,' lamented Frances with unkind truth.

Charles Fleetwood had been recalled from Ireland, and his wife, Bridget, the fourth Cromwell sister, and her five children were back with him. Her last two daughters from her first marriage had been raised solely in Ireland by the amiable hand of their stepfather after the death of their rather stern father, and they'd become as strange and unmanageable as wild Irish colleens.

Even Betty, with her sweet and understanding nature, was put out by them. 'They have such malevolent looks,' she confided to her younger sisters when they came to her bedside to see how she did.

She lay propped up by a mound of pillows to help lessen her stomach pain, and the room was warm and friendly with a good fire in the grate. Beyond the cream damask curtains, drawn against the gloom of the short afternoon of late December, large, silent flakes of snow had begun falling. The cobbles of London's streets, brown with horse-droppings and slithery with discarded refuse, still showed through the thin layer of white, but would soon be covered with the illusion of purity and cleanliness to make every street and square seem wider and more silent.

In her bed Betty pressed her lips against twinges of pain but kept her bright mien. 'They are such strange children. They put me ill at ease, especially the younger one, Bridget. I know not what to say to her. She takes after her father, Ireton. I could never call him Henry. He was a strange man too.'

She twisted a little in her bed, trying to hide the pain. 'It's wrong of me, but I cannot help wishing Bridget and her children had remained in Ireland.'

Mary shrugged. 'Papa couldn't leave Charles Fleetwood out there any longer. I thank God he's such a pleasant and likeable person, but he's not one to manage a country like Ireland. It was a mistake to send him there. The people are too tenacious of their own ways, and still resent us. They need a firm but persuasive rule. Our brother Henry is far more capable. Charles was ever attending Baptist meetings, upsetting the Irish by it.'

'So strange,' mused Betty, 'Bridget's husbands being so different each from the other. Ireton reaped that country's hatred by his unremitting severity and Charles has reaped its contempt by his soft-heartedness. Thank the Lord for our dear brother, who has already gained much respect for his fair-mindedness. I think it's in father's mind to make him Lord Lieutenant. But we must say nothing to Bridget. She'd be so put out . . .'

Her words lost strength as the pain took her again. Sighing, she lay back and the two girls watched her in concern.

'Shall we summon Doctor Goddard?' asked Frances.

Betty shook her head. 'I have some laudanum to ease me.' She gave another harrowing sigh. 'I'll take some now and sleep a little.' She smiled apologetically as they tenderly kissed her cheek and crept away.

If Bridget was disappointed at her husband being replaced, she put on a brave face. 'He was brought home to take control of East Anglia,' she announced haughtily. 'He is now one of His Highness's major generals.'

Frances hid a smirk. It had been a new idea of Papa's after the Penruddock uprising in March, when Royalists and Levellers had joined forces against Parliament. It had been put down quickly enough, but it was a sign of the country's unrest. Cromwell's course against any future uprising had been to carve the country into controllable areas, each under the authority of a major general.

John Lambert controlled the north – his home county was Yorkshire and he had in fact moved there. The Midlands came under Papa's cousin, Edward Whalley, Wales and Herefordshire under James Berry, while William Goffe and Thomas Kelsey had the southern counties, Worsley had Cheshire, Heath in charge of Lincolnshire, Fleetwood had East Anglia, and so on.

Frances felt sorry for Charles. The stern rule of such men wasn't popular with the people, coupled with her father's decision to close all places of public entertainment, cockfighting, bear-baiting, race meetings – anywhere a crowd could conceal a meeting of a more sinister sort. As well as their enforcement of this ruling, the major generals also raised money for the country's constant expenditure, and with the life of the people grown dreary, it was little wonder they were hated, gentle Charles Fleetwood included.

The Protector's popularity too was as low as at any time in his rule. But he remained adamant even when, from her sick bed, Betty tried to plead the people's need for some recreation in their dull lives.

'You are a kind person,' he told her, 'but do not understand the situation. I admit that there is much resentment in the nation of the fact that we must ban our race meetings and our cockfighting. But banned they must be.'

'You cannot make them illegal,' she insisted.

'I have never considered them illegal, merely a temporary measure to prevent them benefiting those who would meet to plot against Parliament. We can never be sure when our enemies will strike again.'

'Meanwhile,' sighed Betty wearily, 'the people are deprived of what little harmless pleasure they have.'

For all his love of her, his face grew tight. 'They have become overfond of pleasure. I would beseech them to keep better employed seeking God more frequently than laying bets at cockfights. Take heed, my dear, I am not against pleasure. Indeed I enjoy mine as much as any man. But it should not be allowed to become a main pursuit in life.'

He got to his feet to leave, but gave one parting shot. 'They shall return to their public entertainments as soon as we think it safe, and not before. Meanwhile, worry yourself no more about affairs of state, but think only on becoming well again. I've been worried to death for the well-being of the sweetest of all my daughters.' And he bent and tenderly kissed her forehead.

Had Betty possessed the smallest bone of spite in her body she'd have condemned him as a hypocrite, for while others' lives grew drearier, life at court became if anything livelier than at any time hitherto as winter passed and the weather improved.

Lacking public diversion, those of good standing with His Highness wheedled invitations to Hampton Court, usually through a close friend or a member of the family, Richard being the main source, his easygoing pursuit of enjoyment attracting friends of the same ilk.

Frances had never seen such gatherings as were at table in the great hall that first weekend in March. Seated at the family table on a raised dais, she could see across the heads and it was like looking at an ocean.

'There must be over a hundred here,' she whispered to Mary as they began the first course of richly flavoured meats and savouries. Later would come the game and lighter meats and sweet stuffs, puddings, custards, fruits, cheeses and sweetmeats.

Mary glanced around as she took a helping of venison in rich sauce. 'I wouldn't have thought that many, but this great place makes any crowd seem few.'

Frances had to agree. The great hall could take a visitor's breath away. More than a hundred feet in length and forty feet in width, the hammer-beam ceiling soared to a height of sixty feet, dwarfing everyone below it. Multicoloured shafts of light poured in from stained-glass windows bearing the badges and arms of Henry VIII, lighting tapestries with brilliance, and glinting off the silver tableware.

'I see Robert Rich is here with Dick,' remarked Mary with her mouth full. 'Such a fashionable young man. See how bravely he dresses? He nigh outdoes our Richard.'

A pang of jealousy surprised Frances. 'You find him so attractive?'

Mary shrugged lightly. 'A little too gallant, I think. Who'd think him the grandson of a Puritan peer, the way he dresses so flamboyantly?'

'I think he dresses most pleasingly,' blurted Frances, regretting her rash defence of him as Mary stopped eating to stare at her in amusement.

'Why, Frankie, I do believe you are taken with him!'

'I'm nothing of the sort!' Frances said tersely and fell to piling food on to her plate, far more than she needed.

From that moment she was all too conscious of Mary's eyes on her as she tried to stop her own from stealing to where Robert Rich sat with her brother and his friends. And all the time she was trying not to look, her heart asked, *What is he doing? Is he looking towards me? Does he hold opinion of me?*'

Each time she dared to look, she was ever more aware of how handsome he was – the generous mouth, the noble forehead, the golden hair curling about broad shoulders, not caught up in any of those silly lovelocks tied with bows as some young men had. He was tall and slim. His face was narrow with high cheekbones, a straight nose and well-spaced, almond-shaped eyes. The more she peeped, the more her heart fluttered, and all the time there was Mary smirking. She could have hit her!

Oliver sat in his Whitehall study with John Thurloe, his personal secretary, sorting through papers for more talks with his Council of State. Money was needed. The Treasury was low. The country was not happy. People were edgy.

This governing without the aid of a parliament wasn't working. His major generals hadn't raised the funds needed to finance England in her conflict with Spain or with problems in Hispaniola and the new Jamaican colony.

He was beginning to foster the suspicion that, as in some earlier parliaments, his major generals had become greedy, keeping back for themselves a good portion of the money they'd raised. He couldn't keep proper check on them, spread as they were across the country. Each a potentate in his little area, not one of them was consistent with another. The lenient Heath was allowing race meetings at Lincoln, while in Cheshire the overzealous Worsley had forbidden them, with severe penalties for any flaunting his authority. The same thing was going on all over the country, causing bad feelings and unrest among the people and, worse still, jealousy between the major generals themselves.

'These men are driving me to the end of my tether,'

Oliver complained to Thurloe. 'They are worse than any parliament, whose petty quarrelling was at least all under one roof, to allow me to keep track of them.'

'Would His Highness consider disbanding them and resorting again to a parliament?' enquired Thurloe, sifting through papers for his employer to sign.

Oliver's reply was sharp. 'I think not.' But his eyes were hollow with defeat. To do what Thurloe suggested would be to admit to another failure of judgement.

A king might do without parliament. Laws had been made by kings, and by kings had been broken. Parliament had merely enforced them, and to break any law made by a sovereign was treason. In his case, however, those laws laid down by a mere Protector, and without the strength of a parliament behind him, could be called into question by anyone in the land.

It had recently been proved. By a certain George Coney, a merchant, who had refused to pay customs duty, stating it had not been imposed by Parliament. Brought to court, the case had been such a bone of contention that, unable to establish the legality of a Protector's imposition of customs duty, Chief Justice Rolle had promptly resigned. Oliver had been made to look foolish, his authority brought down so simply, proving how easily the country could fall into chaos by the lack of proper leadership.

'I've striven, to the wrecking of my own health,' he told Thurloe, 'to bring this land to high esteem in the world. And to what avail? To be reviled and made jest of.'

Thurloe ceased shuffling through papers to look at him, his gaze steady and reassuring. It was as if his secretary had second sight, or else was so close to him as to know his every thought. 'None in all Europe makes jest of you, sir. You are held in greatest respect.'

Yet for all his conviction, Thurloe could never know what it was to rule a land, alone. Oliver gave Thurloe a wry smile.

'I have striven to tolerance in applying laws that will hold this country to greatness. I've shown that tolerance to all religions, so long as there is no blasphemy. I do not persecute the Jews, as have some kings, and I allow Catholics and Quakers alike to practise their extremities of faith so long as it is in moderation, and provided they are circumspect about it. I tell you, John, few kings have allowed what I allow. Yet still it is not enough. A king is one to be feared – a Protector merely worthy of a snook of the nose. Catholics openly condemn us. Baptists are making such a nuisance of themselves that I must dispatch half of them to Ireland to be rid of them. Quakers are such firebrands of speech and action that they cause commotion wherever they go, and it's impossible to send them to Ireland, but they have to be thrown into prisons instead, and branded for their pains.'

He gazed at Thurloe, his eyes misting. 'There are times I wonder why I strive so for this ungrateful nation. How much longer my health will allow it, I do not know. This stone in my insides drives me near mad with its torment. Indeed I do sometimes feel my demise cannot be too distant.'

Sometimes he did feel an old man, and like an old man he turned to any who'd lend an ear to his woes. The best of them was his beloved Betty – she herself ailing, there was more understanding in her than any he knew.

She was reading when he came to her room – an amusing little book in French, whose title translated as *Love's Masterpiece* which belonged to her maid. Hastily she slipped it out of sight under a cushion on her daybed as he came in, her smile bright and innocent as she said how good it was to have the pleasure of his company.

He sat himself in one of her chairs, sighing. 'Not so good company as you might hope for, my dear, but one selfish enough to have need of your bountiful solace.'

She was all attention now. 'How then can I raise your spirits, Papa?'

Again he sighed. 'If you knew the jealousies among us – those major generals, they turn all into gall and wormwood. My heart is for the people, yet so many are repining everything.'

'Try to think of happier things,' she returned. 'Henry and Elizabeth in Ireland are soon to have their first child – let's pray it be a fine healthy son.'

Her mind was on Henry. In a letter to her he'd bemoaned his father's constant interference on how best to rule Ireland, and spoke of a word being said on his behalf to the effect that he did not welcome his father's meddling:

Does he think me a child? I'm advised by him to pray to the Lord to give me a plain simple heart, to take heed of being overzealous lest I cause offence, and not to be too hard on any who contest me. Who does he think I am? I am well loved and respected here. Rather than his needless advice, I more require his support. Nor do I welcome those hordes of Baptists he

27

deports here to be rid of them. I find no pleasure in them.

With this in mind, Betty said, 'I hear Henry is doing well in Ireland. How wise you were to replace Charles Fleetwood with him. I'm certain you can rest assured of Henry's capable rule there. He's well liked and an able commander. I should think he has little need of advice, so capable is he.'

But her words fell on deaf ears as her father stood up wearily, saying she must be tired, and he'd not burden her further with his troubles. Kissing her cheek, he lumbered out leaving her thinking of Henry and wishing she hadn't been so outspoken. Her father leaving so abruptly had her wondering if she might have offended him by it. Even so, Henry's letter gnawed at her, and she did not sleep well that night for thinking about it.

She rose early and made her way to Frances' room, knowing full well that to say anything to Mary would be tantamount to letting the whole palace know. She tapped lightly on the door.

Frankie was already up, still in her wrap, and having her hair dressed by her maid, Marie.

'I've tried my best to intercede for Henry,' Betty said after sharing her worries about him. 'But these matters are for men to resolve. Nor do I have the strength in me to speak for him.'

'He has no right to involve you at all in his petty disagreements,' Frances said angrily. 'Hasn't he sinew enough to speak his mind to Papa without crying to you?'

'He has, but to no avail. Father is blind to anything

that doesn't suit him. But I can no longer support others as once I did.'

'No more should you, low in health as you are.'

Betty gave an apologetic shrug at the reference to her recent invalidity. From the stool where she sat, she watched Mademoiselle Duret brushing her sister's dark ringlets around one slim finger. A girl in her early twenties, petite and artistic, she took joy in her duties, and derived pleasure in teaching Frances to pronounce her French with hardly any English accent.

'In truth,' she confided, 'there are times, Frankie, when I think our father is becoming a little addled in his mind.'

Frances, aware of her sister's lack of caution, turned quickly to her maid. 'I'll breakfast in my room, Marie, if you'd go and ask for something to be brought here. A milk caudle and some toast.'

Betty had fallen silent, aware of her rashness. Even loyal personal maids had ears and tongues to wag, albeit innocently. Gossip gathered in this way was easy for staff to relay to each other, travelling the whole palace and perhaps beyond. The moment she had gone, Betty resumed.

'I have to say what I feel. Father must be aware of Henry's success in Ireland, yet he persists in being at the helm of all things. He seems loath to give Henry credit for anything he achieves, but in the same breath condones Dick's laxities and tolerates his every incompetence. Yet he puts on Dick official responsibilities which as he must know he does not have a gift for. Why give Dick such high office – a man who lets his own bailiff defraud him? Dick can hardly be thought of as a candidate for a political career,

29

yet Father cannot abide seeing Henry the better man politically.'

Frances wished she wouldn't disparage Dick so. He was her favourite brother, and it was hurtful, and she took no time in telling Betty so. For once Betty was unrepentful.

'On the one hand he cautions me against over-exuberance when he knows my health forbids it, and on the other he advises Bridget to be merrier. He even counsels her own husband to see that she is. As to yourself and Mary, he does nothing to seek a suitor for her, yet labours on your behalf – and you the younger – and even then is ever changing course, first fixing on this suitor, then that, and all for naught.'

Frances had to agree. The latest had also been short-lived – the Duke of Enguien, son of the Prince of Condé, who'd led a revolt against the boy King Louis XIV. Papa had been very taken by that anti-Royalist, but European politics soon put an end to that hope – Spain, France and the Netherlands had been alarmed and displeased by the idea of a union between a French dissident and a daughter of the Protector of the British Commonwealth. Trade and finance, it seemed, took precedence over domestic affairs.

Rumours of yet another candidate had come to her ears last autumn, though she wasn't sure whether to be pleased or not. Mama had mentioned it first, and she'd responded quite properly, saying that although she'd not met Charles Stuart, she understood him to be so charming and handsome that all the ladies in France were said to swoon at the sight of him. But there were also stories of the exiled king's debaucheries and endless mistresses, and Frances, saying nothing of these, said that she was pleased and flattered by this tentative proposal, *if* it were sound!

That was enough. Nothing more was said on the subject. She wasn't surprised. It did strike one as incredible that an exiled king, the son of one whose execution her own father had ordered, should wish to marry the daughter of the executioner. She'd shrugged it off as another of her father's whims. That she could become a queen was outweighed by the fact that it would be nicer to marry someone she could truly love – the very handsome Robert Rich, for instance.

Three

L ord Broghill's coach rumbled through the London streets on its way to one of his frequent audiences with His Highness at Whitehall.

Of late he'd been cautiously wooing Cromwell to a more benevolent attitude towards Charles Stuart, and his errand this wet March morning was one of special delicacy.

Gazing at passing Londoners leaning against the chill wind as they went about their business, he contemplated how best to conduct himself before Cromwell's reaction. It was Charles Stuart himself who had first suggested the idea, almost in jest, of being restored to the throne through marriage with one of the Protector's daughters.

The young man had corresponded with him often during his seven-year exile, and Lord Broghill, with both Royalist and Parliamentarian sympathies – whichever suited the times – felt no compunction that his own loyalties faced both ways as a friend to both Charles Stuart and Cromwell. As far as he was concerned, each had his shortcomings and each his finer qualities, and who was he to judge? Except it was better to be on the side of the strongest when the time came to choose.

Cromwell would never allow Charles back on the

throne. But if one of his daughters were to favour a match with the young man – and Broghill's agents had intimated that the youngest did not seem averse to it – then might Cromwell's mind be changed, seeing his own daughter a future Queen of England and the whole Cromwell family legitimately lifted up never to be put down?

The carriage coming to a halt alongside a dozen others outside the Banqueting Hall, he alighted to run the gauntlet of wind and rain to the entrance. There he handed his rain-spattered cloak to a footman in black and silver livery before making his way at a more leisurely pace to the audience chamber.

As always on a Monday, it was crowded with those frustrated at having to kick their heels all week-end until His Highness's return from Hampton Court. Ambassadors and envoys with their ladies, foreign ministers, men of title, men with grievances, men on business – those in fine silks, feathered hats, lace cuffs and tasselled breeches rubbed shoulders with buff- and crimson-coated army officers and dour, black-coated extremist Puritans. But colour far out-did the sombre tones with a scene as rich as any royal court, as, drawn into small groups or pairs, they filled the air with high discussion and earnest debate.

On a gold silk and plum velvet draped dais, a great gilded, ornate chair held the Lord Protector, his dress only slightly improved over the years and still worn without care for his greatness.

Broghill made the usual triple obeisance when his turn came to approach His Highness. He was acknowl-edged with the clownish alacrity Cromwell reserved for his closer acquaintances – a roguish grin and a flourish of the hand, mocking the royal greeting.

Encouraged, Broghill conveyed the hope of speaking with him later on a more social level, and was gratified by Cromwell's rejoinder, 'A tankard or two in my chambers afterwards, my dear Broghill, that we might hear what tidbits of news the City has to offer.'

He found Cromwell lounging in an elbow chair before a blazing fire, smoking his pipe. As he entered, Cromwell laid the pipe across a stand and rose to greet him. 'Ah, my good fellow! Come, sit with me.'

Taking his arm, he led him to a chair opposite his. 'Where have you come from, and what news do you bring?'

'From the City,' replied Broghill in the same jovial manner, heartened as Cromwell poured two silver mugs of ale from a silver jug on the side table without bothering to summon a servant. 'Where I've heard strange news.'

Handing him a tankard, Cromwell sat down again and took up his pipe from its stand. 'And what is this strange news?'

Broghill hesitated. Now it came to it, it wasn't easy. The man's smile looked suddenly strained. 'Yes?' The prompt was evenly said, but a certain command had crept into it, the aura of light-heartedness fading. Broghill strove to correct the situation.

'Perhaps Your Highness will be offended.'

'I will not, be it what it may.'

Broghill forced a light laugh. 'The news is that you are going to restore the king and marry him to the Lady Frances.'

Oliver smiled as though to himself. 'And what do the fools think of it?'

'They like it, and think it the wisest thing you can do – if you can accomplish it.'

'Do you believe it too?' The man was looking steadily at him.

'I do believe it's the best thing you can do to secure yourself,' Broghill stated bravely. He waited while Cromwell drew contemplatively on the long-stemmed pipe, emitting wisps of aromatic smoke.

After what seemed an age, Oliver laid the pipe aside and got up to pace the room with slow, measured steps. Suddenly he stopped. 'Why do you believe it?' he asked, turning on him.

Taken off guard, Broghill tried not to stammer. 'Why . . . nothing could be easier than to bring about the restoration. You'd have the king for your son-in-law and in all probability become grandparent to the heir to the crown. The Lady Frances would be Queen, Your Highness.'

As he spoke, Oliver had returned to his pacing. Now he paused again, gazing at the floor. 'He will never forgive me the death of his father.'

'Sir,' ventured Broghill, 'you were one of many concerned in it, but you will be alone in the merit of restoring his son. Employ somebody, sir, to put it to him, and see how he will take it. I'll do it, if you think fit.'

The Protector's gaze remained preoccupied with the floor. 'No, he will never forgive me his father's death,' he said slowly, then, taking Broghill by surprise, brightened instantly, lifting his head and smiling. 'Besides,' he said in a totally different tone, as though some great burden had been lifted from him, 'he is so damnably debauched!'

Letting out a loud, harsh laugh, he seated himself once more and took up his pipe. 'And now, my dear friend,' he chuckled, 'what think you of my son Henry's administration in Ireland? He appears very much at home there, and the Irish do hold him in some affection, I think.'

With this he slid further into his chair, prepared for a social half-hour with his old comrade-in-arms from their days in Ireland. Thus was the subject of the future of Lady Frances with the exiled king deftly and irrevocably put aside with no chance of the conversation being pushed further.

Undeterred, Broghill applied to the Protectoress.

'Were Your Highness to press him strongly to consider it again . . .' he suggested after acquainting her with the joy such a marriage would give her youngest daughter, at the same time alleviating the Lord Protector of many of his present cares of office as time went on.

She was only too happy to see her husband lightened of his burden, and promised to do what she could. But in the end she too had to admit defeat.

After some weeks she reported sadly to Broghill.

'He never returns me any other answer than that the king is not such a fool as to forgive him the death of his father.'

Frances felt her emotions utterly awash on hearing of the failure of this latest and most illustrious suitor yet.

'I'm like the refuse that floats along on the Thames,' she lamented to Mary. 'I am at the mercy of the currents, pulled back and forth with the flowing in and out of the tide. Papa has reached the pinnacle of his search on my behalf. He can go no higher. I shall never be married!'

'Of course you will,' said Mary. 'Perhaps not so high, but you'll marry eventually.'

Her tone of unmistakable relief revealed a touch of jealousy at the high offer Frances had received, but Frances felt too downcast to care. 'I have been offered a king . . .'

She let the words trail off, realising that her disappointment was not because she had yearned to be wife of a king, but rather that now her future was uncertain. Even an arranged marriage – any arranged marriage – would have settled that uncertainty for good, but now she felt that she was nowhere and nothing.

Through all this her eyes had continued to be drawn to Robert Rich, even dreaming of him in her sleep. But he seemed to treat life so lightly that it was doubtful if he had any serious intentions towards her. It had seemed better with the royal name of Charles Stuart dangling before her to trust her father's wiser judgement, particularly as it was known that he regarded Robert Rich as little more than a gallant with no seriousness to his nature nor any strength of will or stature. Yet she hadn't been able to thrust that face from her mind. And in her mind had been the dilemma – if she refused Charles Stuart in favour of Robert Rich only to have him turn aside from her, how could she go begging that she would accept the royal suitor after all? She'd have lost the greatest opportunity of her life, seldom offered to a commoner. But now, having reconciled herself to allowing her mind to dwell on His Majesty, even to being pleased with that sensuous face, to be told it had come to nothing . . .

'I've half a mind,' she burst out passionately, 'to seek out Master Rich and acquaint him openly with my wish that he pay court to me. We'll see what Papa thinks about that!'

'You wouldn't dare,' said Mary in awe.

'I would. If Papa cannot find me a husband, I shall find my own. He has intervened once too often. But he can hardly intervene between myself and an earl.'

'He has managed to thwart a king.'

'Charles Stuart is king only in exile. But Robert Rich is heir to his grandfather's title. Papa could not insult such an eminent family as the Earl of Warwick's by refusing a marriage contract between his daughter and the heir to that title and fortune.'

In a flurry of excitement at this new ploy, Frances leapt from where she had been sitting. 'And there I have him! Papa will not get out of this so easily, Mall. You'll see!'

Her encounters with Robert Rich had always been in the company of others – frothy, flirtatious little conversations, in keeping with all those young people around her. She'd kept him at a distance while rumour had abounded of the exiled king's interest in her, making sure that this time her head would rule her heart even though that heart grew excited every time Robert came near. There was no Charles Stuart now. She was free to follow her heart.

Parliament breaking for a short recess this last week in March, Frances was delighted when her father decided to venture from the stilted life at Whitehall to the more relaxed atmosphere of Hampton Court.

'Away with dull winter!' he cried, despite it being bitterly cold, with even a threat of snow in the lowering clouds. 'I need to have room to breathe.'

She too needed room to breathe. The dullest weather could not detract from the romantic setting of Hampton Court, with the coming together of young people, and many a love match resulting.

Sunday morning as always was spent listening to sermons, the Royal Chapel kept as plain as its vaulted ceiling with carved and gilded pendants would allow. The great palace might have its tapestries and rich paintings restored, but not here. Gone were the altar and the choir stalls, the organ banished – no canorous music was to desecrate the peace of God's house. The pews had been taken out and plain chairs substituted for family and friends to gather about the ornate pulpit that had been permitted to remain, and the spectator's balcony from the Haunted Gallery still allowed visitors.

Today just a handful of guests were here. The cold weather no doubt. During Doctor Owen's sermon, Frances glanced up at the balcony, and for one heart-stopping moment thought she saw Jerry White standing there in the gloom, his face pale above his black clothes. But a second look revealed only faces she didn't recognise, and, taking a deep breath, she turned her attention back to Doctor Owen, pushing aside that brief moment of hurt and excitement.

Afterwards there would be a modest repast. In the afternoon people would make for their chosen recreation – a quiet table game, a canter through the park for the hardier, or just sitting and chatting the rest of the day away. The evening would bring further diversion, Mary playing fashionable music by Henry Lawes. She'd become very adept at the organ, the lovely one brought to Hampton Court from Magdalen College, no longer having pride of place in church but acceptable for domestic purposes. After her, Frances might take her turn, she too being quite talented.

Sometimes Papa would engage the gifted organist John Hingston, but as there was only a small gathering this weekend it was she and Mary who'd play simpler pieces. Later would come games, dainty sweetmeats handed round, heady wine and hot spicy punch, the ladies hiding their flushed faces behind small practical fans, pretending it to be the huge fire making their cheeks warm.

But that was to come. With midday dinner over, Frances made a beeline to where her brother Dick was laughing with some companions in the watching chamber. Robert Rich was among them.

'Ah, our sweet Frances!' bantered Richard as she came up to them.

'Sweet indeed,' Robert said as he made a great play of kneeling and taking her hand with a flourish that would have been envied by the French king, and brushing it lightly with his lips. But when he raised his eyes to hers she saw no playfulness in them but a depth of esteem that made her blush.

For all his jauntiness he looked less robust than when she had last seen him, a delicate texture to his slightly high colour giving the skin a transparent appearance. But his eyes sparkled well enough.

'I do confess to burning the candle,' he laughed

when she expressed concern for him. 'My tutor, Doctor Gauden, tends to work me hard.'

'You tutor should look more to your health than your scholastic achievements,' she said so severely that he burst out laughing.

'A week or two of idleness will improve me. Tomorrow I visit my grandfather.'

'The Earl of Warwick?' she enquired and he nodded carelessly.

'I saw so little of him while in France with Doctor Gauden, and of late his age is beginning to rail against him so much that I must make some effort to see him more often and cheer him a little.'

'Such it seems with my father also,' Frances said gravely. All this while she had been taking in everything about his looks, intending to commit them to memory and bring them out later in the privacy of her bedchamber to be savoured before she fell asleep to dream of him. 'I commend your consideration of your grandfather,' she added as an afterthought. 'He must cherish you greatly for it.'

'I think so.' He appeared to have become aware of the stuffy air in the watching chamber and his voice had grown soft. 'I think he looks forward to my visits. He lives at Felstead, which is in Essex.'

'My father has estates in Essex.'

'Has he now?' He'd drawn closer to her, isolating her from the rest of the circle of chattering young people. She found herself thinking that even this wasn't enough, that she wished she could be entirely alone with him.

He seemed to read her thoughts as he bent towards her. 'Do you not find it somewhat airless in here?' he asked softly.

'I do indeed,' she answered, her heart beginning to race. 'The fire is too fierce and there are so few windows open. I assume that's because people fear to create a draught, with this weather.'

She had become unaccountably nervous, talking too much. But her mind was racing ahead. Was it imagination that he seemed to be drawing even closer to her?

'I've a mind to take a short ride in the saddle,' he was saying. 'The day has become overcast, but a steady ride would be most exhilarating, though a little boring on one's own. Would I be too presumptuous were I to express a wish of your company?'

Her reply was immediate, but so that her eagerness wouldn't appear too blatant, she made a small, playful curtsy. The gesture caught his sense of humour and he laughed. 'Then it is settled.'

He turned to Richard – now in deep conversation with Richard Beke, an Army officer and son-in-law of Robert's father's sister Catherine – and touched him on the arm to distract his attention a moment. 'Have I your permission for your sweet sister to accompany me for a short canter out to Bushey Park?'

Richard made no hesitation. 'By all means.'

'Then I shall bid her find her gentlewoman as chaperon.'

Dick burst out laughing. 'Why Rob, do you fear that my sister may attempt to sully you?'

There was a sly look on Dick's face and he lowered his tone so that Frances could not hear. 'She is well brought up, sir, but can you not see with half an eye how she gazes at you? So be damned to chaperons!'

It took but a moment for Marie to help her change into suitable outdoor clothing. She found Robert pacing anxiously in the mews, and his relief at seeing her made her heart leap for joy.

'I've horses ready,' he said, with near excitement in his own voice.

The air was crisp with the smell of snow. Sniffing it, the horses lifted their eager heads as they were led out, already saddled, by a shivering groom.

As eager as they to be off, Robert swung easily up after helping her to mount, and they moved off into the park at a gentle walk so as not to alert anyone to the racket of cantering hooves on the cobbles. Frances was glad. If Papa were to be made aware of her intentions, he would have sent out a servant to attend them. Her next hour or so with Robert must be hers alone.

She hardly noticed the cold, and they'd only gone a few hundred yards when snow began to float down on them. Within minutes it had become a steady fall, settling on their shoulders, the folds of their cloaks, their hats, the backs of their gauntlets and on the horses' manes. It was quiet, the grass muffling the sound of a gentle canter, broken only by their horses' breathing – the breath condensing on the cold air – and an occasional snort as one or the other blew its nostrils against a flake of snow.

In the park they passed only one other couple riding back towards the palace. They acknowledged Frances from afar with a brief wave, but soon all became still and silent again, as though no other living soul shared the world with them.

Turning off the broad swath on to a narrower bridle path between the trees, putting distance between themselves and the palace, they spoke little, a comment or two, no more, Robert asking if all was well with her, was she tired, to tell him when she wished to slow or stop to rest, and she assuring him of her perfect well-being. All the time a peculiar anticipation churned deep inside her, a feeling she hadn't experienced since her episode with Jerry White, whose memory now struck her as most unpalatable.

Robert was far removed from all Jerry White had been. He struck her as sensitive, thoughtful, pure in heart, for all his light manner, and certainly not the gallant he made himself out to be in public. He was gentlemanly and considerate, and she had no fear of his ever forcing himself upon her as Jerry had done, or taking advantage of her for his own gratification.

From time to time she stole glances at him from beneath the narrow brim of her hat, each time experiencing a surge of admiration at the fresh and open expression. No smouldering sensuality here, as had been . . . She could not even let her mind form that man's name now.

Every now and again, as though he felt her eyes on him, Robert glanced across at her, and as their glance met he smiled – such a smile that she knew he was in love with her. It was all happening so quickly.

Her horse snorted as another snowflake entered its nostrils. She leaned forward and patted its neck. The movement caught Robert's attention and he regarded her enquiringly.

'This has become quite a heavy downfall,' he said. 'Will you turn back or shall we shelter for a while until it lessens? There perhaps?' He indicated a small clump of coppiced beeches to one side of the path, the bare branches entwined with evergreen ivy to form a shelter of sorts.

His gaze had travelled to a slightly lighter break in

the clouds to the east, typical of snow showers. 'This shouldn't last overly long,' he said.

With their mounts tethered to a nearby tree, they sat within the circle of saplings, shielded by the substantial growth of ivy, to watch the flakes drift down beyond their refuge – two people, silent ghosts in a silent world on a grey afternoon. He had spread his cloak on the ground, and, sitting close to him, she could feel the warmth radiating from his body, and when he turned to ask if she were warm enough, his breath was sweet and wholesome. She felt herself tremble. It was his closeness rather than the cold, but instantly his arm came about her, drawing her even closer.

'Come, Frances, I'll keep you warm.' His voice was a whisper.

Letting herself lean against him, her very bones seemed to be melting with the pleasure of contact, a most delicious sensation to be savoured while it would last. For a moment or two they sat, not speaking, merely watching the snowflakes drift gently down.

When he spoke again his voice was as low as ever it could be, as if loath to disturb the sense of quiet. 'I am in love with you, Frances.'

That was all, nothing more, but it was enough. This was the man she would marry, who would gladly be hers, seeking no wealth or privilege – for he already had those – and therefore his love was honest.

Her voice strangely shy, she answered, 'I love you too, Robert.'

His next words, though taking her by surprise, were those she had longed for all her life. 'Frances, my dearest, would you consent to become my wife?'

And, closing her eyes to hold her assent that little bit longer, she whispered, 'Oh, yes, Robert.'

Gently he lowered his face to hers. His lips touched hers, pressing lightly, lingering as she clung to him, the breath from her nostrils trailing a thin mist on the cold air while the breath from his was like a tiny warm caress across her cheek.

Her arms wound about him and she pulled him down upon her. Yet it was all so wonderfully calm, his needs restrained out of care for her. No clawing hunger, rather a sweet sense of contentment, as after an answered prayer. A contentment that she knew would come again and again for the rest of their lives together.

Four

1656–57

Henry sat reading Mary's letter. She'd obviously written it in haste, hardly giving herself time to date it properly, merely 'Mid-June fifty-six', her signature a mere scrawl, and even the wax seal an untidy mess.

How Mary loved a scandal. He could imagine her dropping hot sealing wax everywhere in her haste to catch the messenger. Smiling, he read it to his wife.

> I must confess myself in great fault for not writing to you for so long, but you cannot be ignorant of the reason – the business of my sister Frances and Mr Rich. These three months I think our family and myself in particular have been in the greatest confusion and trouble as ever a poor family can be in . . .

Again he smiled. Mary was ever prone to overstress things. The problems of the family hardly touched him here in Ireland. He and Elizabeth were deliriously happy in their Dublin home. Their first son Oliver, born in March, was already the strongest, handsomest, most robust child there ever was, holding up his head on a sturdy neck to gaze about out of large blue eyes so like his mother's.

To celebrate, they'd given a ball, with music, dancing and fireworks. Good wishes had poured in from all over Dublin, and the friends they'd made flocked to see him, while gifts had rolled in as readily as the waves at the mouth of the River Liffey. London and the rest of the family, with their endless troubles, seemed far away.

Yet he couldn't help feeling sorry for Frances. According to Mary, she was having a miserable time of it on account of the problems she and Robert Rich were encountering, as Mary was explaining:

> After a quarter of a year's admissions, Papa and Lord Warwick began to treat about the estate, and my lord offered what Papa expected. The trouble I think is not so much the estate as from private reasons that Papa disclosed to none but Frances and his own family – a dislike for the young man which he had from some reports to his being a vicious man given to play and such things, which office was done by some that had a mind to break the match.

Henry stopped reading to glance across at Elizabeth. 'Our enemies would stoop to anything to discredit us in any way they can, even to the misery of poor Frankie, who's done no harm.'

Elizabeth was sitting by the window playing with her son in his cradle. Rocking the crib gently, she gave Henry a deep look. 'His Highness should take no note of such cruel slander, but consider more his daughter.'

Henry returned to scanning the page. 'It does seem

that our Frances has made a stand. She has found all
the reports raised against Robert Rich to be false.' He
bent his head to read the rest of Mary's letter:

> They were so much engaged in affection that she
> couldn't think of breaking it off, so my sister had
> me and our friends speak on her behalf to Papa,
> which we did, but he would not hear us except to
> promise that if he were satisfied as to the report,
> the estate should not break because of it. Which
> my sister was satisfied with.

It needed concentration to unpick Mary's complicated
way of writing – as complicated, it seemed, as was the
whole business at home – but it was clear that Frances
was the unhappiest girl in all London, and Henry's heart
went out to her.

The Earl of Warwick was obviously keen on a match,
and had asked what was it His Highness wanted more,
promising to do his utmost to satisfy him on all counts.
His Highness had made new proposals, which Lord
Warwick answered as much as he could. But now,
according to Mary, there was quite a bit of money
in trust in the hands of Robert's own father, Lord
Rich, which the man had power to sell – £500 a
year in fact. It seemed that some people had per-
suaded His Highness that it would be dishonourable
for him to conclude the match without that £500 a
year being settled on young Robert on his father's
death. Apparently Lord Rich had no esteem for his
son and refused to agree to it, and His Highness
was convinced that to yield on these terms would
be to show himself as being made a fool of by Lord

Rich. 'Which how that should be I cannot understand,' Mary wrote.

'Nor can I,' Henry muttered, annoyed with his father's usage of poor Frances to justify his own pride.

Resolved to write to Frances telling her to pursue her heart's desire through thick and thin, he mused over the final words of Mary's letter: 'I must tell you privately that they are so far engaged as the match cannot be broken off.'

Wise to the ways of the world and the power of love, he had little illusion as to what that meant. Even for a girl so soundly raised in a Puritan household, it couldn't be a mere matter of holding hands and gazing into one another's eyes. Henry felt deeply sad.

Frances lay huddled in the curve of Robert's arm as they lay within the secret grove that had been theirs since that wintry March day. An August sun now glinted down in flashes of gold through a full canopy of leaves that rustled in the slightest of breezes.

Many people were about on this fine afternoon, but this spot remained undiscovered by all except deer – especially when others were in their beds at night. Many were the hours the two had spent here, some happy, some despairing, when marriage seemed altogether unattainable. Today was one such.

'My father will never relent,' Frances sighed against Robert's shoulder. 'There are times I think he must dislike me utterly, else why cause me such unhappiness?'

He leaned over and lovingly kissed her eyelids. 'He doesn't hate you, my heart. Rather he loves you too dearly, and that is our undoing. For he would shield you from all, even from me, to keep you unharmed by the world. He little realises the harm he himself does you. Be patient, sweetest. We'll win over his loving consent in time.'

His lips touched hers as weightlessly as an alighting butterfly. She closed her eyes and sighed with pleasure as the lips travelled to her throat and on to the unblemished flesh released by his careful opening of her bodice. They'd have made love but for a sudden coughing attack that forced him to turn his head away. Concerned for him, Frances sat up as he strove to suppress the spasm.

'My dear,' she said. He'd been caught by a similar attack a little earlier that day.

'A summer chill,' he excused, recovering. 'It will be gone in a day or two.'

But the moment was lost while he reassured her that the attack was nothing more than a small chill, and indeed when they met again he was quite better, though a slight cough lingered with him all through that autumn and on into the winter.

It had been more than a year since she and Robert had first met, yet nothing had been settled on any marriage contract, her father seeming to find one excuse after another to delay it.

'I begin to think he is jealous,' she told Robert. 'He doesn't want me to marry, ever.'

'Why shouldn't he wish you to marry?' Robert smiled at her but she refused to be mollified.

'I've heard of fathers being jealous of their daughters and looking to guard them against any who would take them from them.'

'That's nonsense, my dear heart,' he laughed, but some distant words of Papa's echoed in her head – *a foolish jealousy for that fortunate man, whoever he will be* – said even as he'd endeavoured to match her with that vapid William Dutton.

It was about then that he'd changed from the father she'd known as a child, the benign man who'd dandled her on his knee and whom she had so adored, yet who became cynical and calculating enough to set spies on her. Perhaps he'd always been that way, the thinly veiled benignity falling away as the years had passed to reveal the hard man of politics and parliaments.

Only this Christmas had he come home in a rage, throwing off his cloak and roaring, 'Such thin attendance! These fine Members of Parliament are more eager to stay at home than attend the House. Christmas Day is becoming as pagan as once it was!'

He had totally ignored her when she tried to lay a comforting hand on his arm, almost to the point of throwing off her hand.

Perhaps he'd had a right to be furious. Last September had seen the inception of his Second Protectorate Parliament, to whom he'd immediately been obliged to turn for money after his major generals had failed to raise it. Seeing themselves taking second place to this new parliament, they had become estranged from him – men such as Desborough, his own brother-in-law, Edward Whalley, his cousin, and John Lambert, once his close friend. Even so, it didn't excuse him pushing her aside the way he had, as though she had never meant anything to him.

'I'm not interested in their quarrels,' she told Betty.

'All I want is an answer from Papa regarding myself and Robert.'

From her bed, Betty had sighed her sympathy. 'You must bide your time, Frankie.' Four months pregnant, her condition had made her ill, and at times she looked as worn out as though already beset by her labours. 'Our poor father looks so careworn these days. If you press him too hard on your own worries, he might turn against the both of you altogether.'

Too worn down by her own ill health, this was all the counsel she could give, and all Frances could reply with was a peevish, 'I'm as nothing to him these days!'

With the spring, talk of kingship came up again. 'A Crown for Cromwell' tripped well off the tongue – a crown made of Spanish gold, after the capture of the Spanish treasure fleet last autumn.

Yet for all the talk of his supremacy, one incident among several proved that he didn't have it all his way with Parliament; the incident – the Naylor affair.

James Naylor, an extreme Quaker, had been going about preaching his blasphemies. His unkempt beard and long flowing hair made followers liken him to Jesus Christ, a blasphemy in itself. With the old problem arising as to whether a protector had the right to try a subject, Naylor was condemned to be whipped through the streets, pilloried, his tongue bored through and the letter 'B' branded on his forehead before being flung into prison.

Frances felt her father's powerlessness in the situation. Despite his effort to show leniency by arranging for money to be sent to Naylor to persuade him to repent his ways, a gesture Naylor churlishly spurned, it proved that for all its talk of kingship, Parliament was quite prepared to ignore his authority when the occasion called. Just as noticeable was Parliament's dismissal of Cromwell's major generals. Not that he had any faith left in them, but his experiment had failed. Even Betty's husband, John Claypole, who he had made Master of the Horse, had been one of their main attackers.

Frances felt he was losing many of his old comrades, though others remained true, such as General Monck, a big, bluff man still in command of Scotland – to the chagrin of Bridget, who had expected that command to be given to her husband on the disbanding of the major generals. It had led to hard feelings at home, although, as Oliver pointed out, a man who couldn't adequately manage Ireland would be of little use in Scotland.

Her father's choice of companions sometimes struck Frances as alarming, the ingratiating Jeremiah White being one. She occasionally caught glimpses of him and often wondered if Papa had retained him only to remind her of her earlier escapade, especially when his ready wit brought a passing smile to her father's face, making her seethe with shame and embarrassment.

Thurloe too still lurked, his spies lately having exposed three recent attempts on her father's life. Astute servant that he was, he chose to enlighten a shocked Parliament on them at the exact time when it was flaunting his employer's authority. It worked as he knew it would, and the appalled Members instantly flocked to their esteemed leader's side hearing of a Royalist plot by a certain Colonel Saxby, a one-time Leveller, to be carried out by one Miles Sindercombe with two others, Boyes and Cecil.

The first plot had been to blow off His Highness's head with a blunderbuss shot from an upper room of a house belonging to a Colonel Mydhope as Oliver passed beneath on his way to Hampton Court. It had been foiled when Thurloe advised going by river; and a second attempt to assassinate him in Hyde Park had apparently been abandoned. The third, to set fire to his apartments at Whitehall, was discovered after one of the Protector's own lifeguards in their pay took fright and exposed them. Cecil immediately confessed, but Sindercombe took arsenic before the eyes of his judges to escape the obscenities reserved for the public execution of traitors.

Despite Parliament's horror of these threats on his person, Oliver became jubilant.

'We must give thanks to the Lord for the safe delivery of His humble servant,' he told them. 'A service of thanksgiving will be held at the Banqueting Hall, which will be opened to the public.'

Frances and Mary watched with pleasure as on the twenty-third of January the Banqueting Hall filled, hundreds inside and still people filing in, all heads lifted to see the painted ceiling and lavishly decorated walls. Spectators jostled important guests, ignoring efforts to keep them at a distance. Up the staircase they crowded, along with friends of the Protector, and even a relative or two, unable to go up or down for the crush. As for her father, he was happier than Frances had seen him in a long time.

'Now's the time to speak to him of myself and Robert,' she said to Mary. 'Before the service begins.'

'Would that be wise, with so many people here and Papa so happy, to spoil his happiness now?' Mary questioned, but Frances was adamant.

'Why should it? Seeing that it's his daughter's happiness we speak of.'

57

She'd waited long enough. Bidding Robert stay behind, she made her way to where her father stood with a small group of friends and their ladies near the newly erected pulpit. Seeing her, his face lit up even more.

'Upon my word!' he surveyed her clear young face and her cerise velvet gown with its yellow taffeta petticoat. 'I do sometimes forget what a charming young woman my little wench has become.'

Thrusting compliments aside she launched straight into her quest. 'Papa, Robert Rich and I have been in love with each other these twelve months. You've treated with my Lord Warwick on our behalf and for that we are both grateful. I do understand Robert's father has been so inconsiderate as to—'

He stopped her with his fingers coming against her babbling lips. 'We are in company, my little one,' he reminded, his tone benign, his mouth smiling. 'This is not the time to air family differences or name names.'

He was leading her as far from his company as the crowds allowed. 'The Almighty has seen fit to spare my life three times, a sure sign of His regard for His servant, that I should continue to care for our nation. But if I cannot find a little time to give some consideration to my own daughter then I shall be remiss indeed. So I will do all I can to grant her heart's desire . . .'

A loud creaking and groaning of stressed timber cut across his words. Seconds later came the sound of splintering wood, of terrified screams and cries followed by an almighty crash as the whole structure of the staircase gave way under the weight of people on it.

There came a general mad surge of helpers towards the wreckage, from which clouds of dust rose to settle on faces and clothes. The victims had been flung down and beneath the jagged remains of treads, risers and splintered banisters, while others had jumped clear. There was hardly room to move as the injured were dragged from ruin into mêlée. Half-fainting, weeping women were led away, struggling through the pack, hair white with plaster, clothing ripped, dust-caked arms and shoulders streaked crimson.

Oliver was standing transfixed by the horror of what he saw.

'Richard,' Frances heard him whisper, and realised that moments before, Dick had been on the stairs. She felt suddenly sick. How many dead in the collapse? Where was Dick?

In seconds her father had recovered. 'Remain here!' he ordered, and pushed through the throng issuing commands, taking charge of a situation that was threatening to become a useless mêlée of would-be helpers. But Frances had seen that stricken look, the lines of fear that had appeared on his face, making him look suddenly very, very old.

In her own panic she ignored his order, began pushing forward and at the same time dreading what she might find. Robert was already there helping a sobbing woman to her feet, her ripped gown and petticoat revealing a full length of leg for all to see. Frances saw him gather the tattered edges of the gown together to hide her shame from onlookers as he carried her to a vacated chair and set her down. Frances felt her heart swell with pride at his thoughtfulness, but there was no time to linger on it.

As Robert returned to help move upended splintered wood, she clutched at his arm. 'Richard – he was on the stairs!' she gasped.

It was then she saw a dozen people dragging aside part of a baluster and to her joy the figure of Richard was being pulled out from under it. She managed to claw her way through to him as he got shakily to his feet, even laughing in an embarrassed manner.

'Oh, Dick, you are hurt,' she fussed as he bade for a hand to help him away to recover somewhat. He had a badly cut and bruised leg but was able to hobble off as order was gradually restored, the injured taken away to be attended to.

Miraculously, no one had been killed, and injuries were relatively light. After some good while the service was able to go on, but now with prayers of thanks added for the rescue of Lord Richard, though Royalists were quick to predict it as yet another sign of the ultimate downfall of the usurper Cromwell.

For Frances the incident had frustrated any hope that day of persuading her father to give further consideration to her and Robert's future.

'It's becoming ever more difficult to approach him,' she complained to Mary. 'He's becoming so drawn in on himself.'

But for the collapse of that staircase she might have had the answer she sought, but since the accident he'd again withdrawn into one of his strange moods of isolation.

'This business of kingship is worrying him,' Mary staunchly defended, and Frances had to agree. Although she fretted about her own future, deep down she knew her father's future was of greater importance. Even so, it irked.

Five

Frances gazed down from one of Whitehall's high windows at Horse Guard's Parade, with St James's Park beyond, all bright in the early morning sun. The sixth of May, Wednesday – another empty, purposeless day.

She had felt this way since her father's reply on the matter of Robert had been interrupted by the staircase incident. He'd still not given her an answer, having far more impending decisions to make, drawing ever further into himself by his continuing indecision on the matter of kingship.

'Oh, here you are!' Mary's voice made her jump. She saw Mary wandering towards her. 'Why are you moping up here all by yourself?'

Her first irritation at being disturbed from her reverie fading, Frances sighed and allowed her sister to join her. 'I was thinking, why cannot Papa make up his mind one way or other to accept Parliament's offer and have done with it.'

To have done with it, for her, meant to refuse its offer. Were he to accept it, it would mean an end to her and Robert's future together, for she would no longer be a commoner and free, but a true princess, forbidden to marry just any man. While Papa continued to vacillate between yes and no to Parliament's invitation to take up the crown, it left some hope, but the waiting was fraying her nerves.

'Four months!' she burst out to Mary. 'Four months and I still do not know where we stand. I'm beginning to be made ill by it, and poor Robert seems not at all well from the strain of waiting. He is forever plagued by his cough. It can only be the nervousness of waiting. It's been a most horrible four months for us both.'

In February, a Member of Parliament and former Mayor of London, Sir Christopher Packe, had presented a weighty document called 'The Humble Address and Remonstrance' calling for a decision on the monarchy. There had been worry ever since the Penruddock revolt, when Penruddock said he wouldn't have lifted a hand against him if Cromwell had been king, because it would have been treason. This just demonstrated again how precarious was the role of Cromwell as merely Lord Protector.

From that moment, her father was besieged by those for and against kingship. At supper one evening with his family, he'd heartened Frances by saying to them all, 'I love not the title of king.'

She found out later that she'd misinterpreted his remark. He did not like the title of king, but the *office* of king was another matter. How else could the country be led forward in peace, the Instrument of Government upheld and the work of the Lord go forward? Such words quickly gained support from those who'd previously opposed him. His position looked positive. Yet with even the Army beginning to see the hand of God in it, the man himself continued to dither as only Cromwell could.

There were opponents too, and for once Frances blessed the dour Bridget and her husband, who had always been against her father taking up a royal sceptre. John Desborough, married to Papa's sister Jane, also stood with Charles Fleetwood, both declaring they deplored his becoming king but would stand by him should he take up any other title, including one that could become hereditary. Lambert wasn't so generous-minded – a seasoned soldier and once right-hand man of Cromwell, he'd hoped to take over on the Protector's death. Not so now. A hereditary title would go to Cromwell's son Richard, and he would be relegated to a nobody.

Listening to all this, Frances had felt in such a state that she was snapping at everyone, even poor Robert.

'I'm becoming inclined to think you've no desire to marry me,' she pouted. 'Else you'd go and say to my father man to man that you'd die rather than lose me, as I would die rather than lose you.'

He'd looked steadily at her. 'That is truer than you think, Frances. I *would* rather die than lose you.'

The simple loving statement had torn at her heart, and she'd thrown herself into his arms, hearing his voice tremble with emotion as he held her close. 'I *will* have you for my wife, Frances, come what may.'

It was hard to imagine how that would ever be, if a monarch decreed it would not be. A king could quite legally annul a marriage, have the husband imprisoned and be within his rights to compel the woman into marriage with another of his own choice. Would her loving father resort to such?

On the thirty-first of March, at the Banqueting Hall, the speaker of the House of Commons officially offered

Cromwell the kingship. At home, Frances had waited
on a knife's edge for the moment when the Humble
Petition and Advice, as it was now called, was handed
to her father to accept the title and office of king.
She'd breathed a sigh of relief that he had given no
proper reply but in a protracted speech had said that
although the immensity of the offer ought to beget in
him a reverence and fear of God, the thing was of the
greatest weight of any that was ever laid upon a man.
Considering such weight, he had begged to be given
time to deliberate and consider what particular answer
he might give to so important a business and to ask
counsel of God and his own heart.

For Frances it had been no answer, but she dared
not cling to hope, for to be disillusioned would have
destroyed her.

March slid into April with her father continuing to
refer to his doubts, his fears, his scruples. Lord Broghill
proclaimed that the law knew no protector, but the nation
loved a monarchy. Fleetwood and Desborough were
still trying to dissuade him, and John Lambert went into
a sulk. And all the while came lengthy speeches from
Cromwell himself to the effect that so far he'd found
their arguments inconclusive, and that Parliament must
find another title, and he did not think God would bless
him for undertaking anything that would grieve them.

'I do not think the thing necessary,' he told Elizabeth.

'Then tell them so,' she replied artlessly, 'and let us
get on with our lives.' She too was petrified of the
repercussions the title of king would have, though for
her it was solely because of a dire need for a simple
life, and for once she was no comfort to him.

Further delays, with him falling prey to ill health,

left the family, the nation and the world in suspense. All this time, Frances tried to cling to hope, while her father more or less divorced himself from his family, excusing himself from most meals, pacing his chambers and going to bed long after they'd all retired.

Today had found him still asking questions of Parliament regarding a droll remark from Colonel Hewson that Parliament must be worse than the Devil, for the Devil had offered Christ the kingdoms of the world only the once, whereas Parliament had so far done it twice!

Turning away from the window, Frances made her way abruptly back to her room, trailed after by Mary. With Mary going off to her own room, she submitted herself to the bright attention of her maid Marie, who was waiting to help her dress into something more suitable for the day.

'How lucky you are, Marie,' she murmured as the girl finished doing her hair for her, 'to be what you are and have no cares.'

'Pardonnez-moi, dame?' Marie enquired prettily. 'Qu'est-ce que vous avez dit?' But Frances shook her head.

'Nothing of importance, Marie,' she sighed, and went down to join the rest of the family for breakfast, feeling that her misery would never end.

Papa came to the table unusually sprightly. He'd almost recovered from his bout of illness, and for once was dressed, rather than in his old gown and slippers. He spoke of having had an informative dinner with Fleetwood and Desborough the previous evening.

'Upon my word!' he laughed as he buttered his bread, helping himself to a slice or two of cold beef. 'They did warn me that if I accepted the kingship I would infallibly draw ruin upon myself and my friends. But I shall prove them misguided, you shall see.'

'Does that mean you will accept?' enquired Elizabeth in a defeated tone.

'It may well be,' came his hearty reply, but he refused to enlarge on that for the rest of the morning, leaving Frances also down in spirit.

Later, he took a stroll in St James's Park, taking advantage of the fine afternoon, and telling everyone that he had at last made up his mind, and that he was arranging to let his decision be known the very next day.

For Frances it was the final blow to any hope of marrying Robert. She wasn't to know that Fleetwood, Desborough and Lambert had followed her father into the park to tell him of their intentions not to oppose him if he accepted the crown, but that if he did they would resign. It was a threat that sent him home a more thoughtful man.

The following day at eleven o'clock, the Committee came together to meet the Protector in the Painted Chamber. But his message was that he could not attend them now but would do so that evening with his firm answer. That evening found the Committee again hovering about at Whitehall long after the House had risen, with no sign of His Highness. Even his family was on thorns as he lounged about in their apartments making no effort to go to the meeting.

Elizabeth was beside herself. 'What do you expect them to do?' she berated, her agitated fingers whipping her embroidery needle in and out of a sampler she was making. 'You cannot keep them kicking their heels so long while . . . *oh*!' She broke off with a cry as the needle caught her thumb.

From where Oliver sat in the small converted parlour, once part of a huge stateroom, before Elizabeth had got at it, he smiled benignly. 'I received delivery of a Barbary horse today – a splendid animal. I ought to go and make certain it is being well tended.' But as he heaved himself out of his chair, she frowned at him whilst she sucked delicately at her pricked thumb.

'You have already inspected it once today.'

'And must needs to again,' he added quietly. 'If it is not well cared for it will sicken and die, whereas this nation has waited this long without hurt to proclaim me King Oliver and can wait a day or two more, I imagine.'

With a small gesture of gallantry he took her hand and gave the hurt thumb a brief kiss before lumbering out of the room, leaving her to press her lips together in exasperation.

The waiting delegation was fortunate enough to catch a glimpse of him as he passed through the chamber on his way to the mews, and sent one of its members to fetch him back. He stared at them all in surprise.

'I sent a message to the House, I'm certain of it. I assumed it was received after the House had risen, and no envoys were sent to me.'

'But we are here,' came the aggrieved reply. 'And have attended very long.'

Almost casually he replied with an apology for the inconvenience they had been put to, graciously thanking them for having waited so long. 'I will meet with you tomorrow at eleven of the clock,' he finished and went off to see his new horse, leaving them to await his answer the next day, which he promised them faithfully would be his final answer.

*   *   *

'What a shame poor Betty cannot be with us,' Frances remarked, as the small flotilla bore the family upriver to Westminster Steps, the boatman rowing mightily on a slack tide. 'She will miss everything.'

Her father smiled fondly at her. He looked quite splendid in a suit of deep crimson. 'Betty is safer remaining at home. She has not the strength to be out of bed with the baby so soon due.'

But Frances was too excited to worry unduly about Betty.

It was the twenty-sixth of June, a glorious Friday afternoon. Papa's investiture would take place at two o'clock at Westminster Hall. Soon they were tying up beside the steps and being helped out by the boatman, who was cleanly attired for the occasion, while dignitaries greeted the Cromwell family with formal handshakes and courteous bows.

Whilst the rest went on into Westminster Hall, Cromwell met with his Council of State to give formal assent to the now modified Humble Petition and Advice before he too returned to Westminster Hall for the investiture proper.

The crowds were treated to a procession as grand as the coronation of King Charles had been, which many still remembered. Preceded by his gentlemen-in-waiting, heralds, the King of Arms and Garter, the Earl of Warwick and the Lord Mayor of London bearing the Sword of the City, His Highness came on, followed by judges and aldermen of the City of London and the officers of his Army.

Inside the hall, filled to capacity with Members of Parliament, people of quality and ambassadors from all over Europe, the dais on which the coronation chair stood was draped with pink Genoese velvet edged with gold fringes. Above the throne hung the Cloth of State. Before it a table was laid with a great gilt-embossed bible, a Sword of State and a sceptre of solid gold. Nearby lay a robe of purple velvet edged with ermine.

Frances watched as her father was duly robed, the sword buckled on, the sceptre ritually handed to him. She heard his deep, somewhat harsh voice fill the hall as he uttered the solemn oath, one not far removed from that of an anointed king.

But there had been no anointing, and a crown was absent. When the trumpets sounded, proclaiming him Chief Magistrate of the Three Kingdoms, the shout that went up was not 'God Save the King' but 'God Save the Lord Protector'.

For on that fateful eighth of May 1657, his final answer to Parliament had been, 'I cannot undertake this government with the title of king.' And as if it made a difference, he had apologised to them all for the length of time he had taken in giving them an answer but that it had been a weighty business.

'Frankie!' Mary burst in on her in high excitement. 'It's settled! My wedding will be in the autumn.'

Frances put down the book she was reading. 'I'm so happy for you.'

'I shall be Lady Fauconberg,' laughed Mary, her sister's automatic smile going totally unnoticed. 'Think of it, Frankie. Lady Fauconberg!'

'And do you love him?'

'Oh, I do! I loved him from the very moment we met each other.'

'That was hardly a month ago. Not all that long in which to be so certain.'

The thought of her own long drawn-out romance with Robert went through her mind. But it was possible to fall in love from that very first glance. It had happened to her – twice. One to come to nothing, the other . . . She forced her thoughts from that, and gazed affectionately at Mary.

'I am so glad for you,' she said, but Mary was already gushing on like a spring from which a granite plug had been drawn.

'It would have been settled sooner but for Papa being so beset by concerns of kingship. But that's done with and he has time for us again. He has high esteem for Thomas. He praises both his manners and his education, his fine person and winning behaviour, and his alliances and knowledge of travel and connections, and—'

'Yes, yes!' Frances held up a hand to put a stop to this rush of praise. For this past month Mary had done nothing but talk about her suitor, leaving Frances feeling bleak and forsaken. Nothing had ever been said in this way about Robert, except to swerve aside from any mention of him. But that was not Mary's fault, and she gave her an indulgent smile.

'Sir William Lockhart, our ambassador in Paris, speaks of him as a person of extraordinary parts, and John Thurloe expounds upon his sobriety and applauds his being placed in the new House of Peers, such high qualities does he have.' This last she tried to deliver affectionately, hating the bitter edge that had crept in.

Thomas Bellasyse Viscount Fauconberg was indeed a man of fine qualities. He was charming, and openly treated Mary with loving tenderness, and she felt her heart yearn to enjoy that same openness with Robert as Mary could exhibit with Thomas.

Although only twenty-four or five, Fauconberg was a widower, his late wife Mildred, co-heir of Viscount Castleton, having died after three years of childless marriage, leaving him quite alone in the world. He'd gone abroad to Italy to nurse his loss but on his return had taken up his life again. It was at court that Mary first met him.

It was hurtful to Frances that within weeks of their meeting, Papa had readily granted Thomas Mary's hand in marriage, yet still hedged over Frances and Robert. True, Thomas already possessed his fortune, whereas Robert must wait upon his father's good graces for his. Thomas already enjoyed his title, while Robert wouldn't gain his until his ageing grandfather and his ailing father both expired. The way Frances felt, that could take years. On the other hand, when it did happen, Robert would be an earl, while Thomas would always be a mere viscount. So why couldn't Papa see that, when he had set his mind successfully to so many other things?

The crown of course was now as far removed as ever it could be, and by his own doing. There was no longer talk of royal bridegrooms, so it seemed quite senseless for him to demur any further over Robert. On this she intended making her feelings very clear to him.

Once more she began harassing him. In this, Mary, now familiar enough with the force of love to know just how she suffered, became her greatest ally. Betty too, for all her dreadful health lately, pleaded and cajoled him on her behalf as only she could, with her poignant face and her soulful, hooded eyes, his favourite daughter and now mother of his newest grandson, born within a week of his inauguration.

Richard and Dorothy had taken her side, Mama too, as well as every friend Betty could possibly find to speak on her behalf. By this time she had got herself into quite a state over it, and Robert had also been made quite ill because of it all.

Then suddenly, a week after Mary's news, it came out of the blue. After all her pleading and all the pleading of her family and friends, without warning, her father nodded his consent and gave his blessing. She and Robert would be married.

Six

Mary swung excitedly about the room in her joy. 'We could have a double wedding.'

'I never gave thought to that,' Frances laughed. The dismal past was far behind her. 'What date did you have in mind for yours, Mall?'

Her sister stopped prancing about to regard her with a contemplative smile, her lips parting to reveal small, white, even teeth, and Frances thought she had never looked on so pretty a girl as Mall.

The lips closed on a sudden decision. 'November. It should be in November.'

'Why November? It's such a dull month.'

'Simply because it *is* such a dull month – a wedding will enliven it. And because arrangements must be made that will take time. And because a certain goodly time must elapse or people will begin to tittle-tattle that there must be a reason why I am being hastened into marriage so fast, and . . . because I could not bring myself to wait until the following spring.'

She finished on a rush that made Frances burst out laughing again.

'Then November it shall be,' she cried out in pure joy of life.

*   *   *

Looking back on it, if her father had refused to sanction her marriage, Frances knew she would have been prepared to dare his wrath and run off with Robert to marry him. But an event in September proved what folly that would have been. It also brought home the fact that though her father might not be a king, his power was every bit as awesome.

He'd never quite forgiven the high-stomached Duke of Buckingham, George Villiers, for having spurned her, and true to character, Cromwell had patiently bided his time until providence gave an opportunity for restitution.

Some time ago, George Villiers had cast his eye in the direction of the daughter of the retired Sir Thomas Fairfax. She had been promised to the Earl of Chesterfield, and banns had already been twice published. So it caused quite a scandal when Mary Fairfax, having fallen deeply in love with Villiers, eloped with him to Bolton Percey in Yorkshire, and was married on the seventh of September, despite Cromwell's intervention.

Frances was enlightened to all the facts by her ever informative sister, already drawing on the business as a leech draws on the vein of a sick man's arm.

'Papa has never forgiven Thomas Fairfax for his cowardly withdrawal from the Scottish campaign,' Mary said darkly. 'It was because of him that Papa had to leave us all and go off on that awful expedition. He never quite regained his health because of it. And now with George Villiers marrying Mary Fairfax after spurning you as he did, no wonder Papa is outraged.'

'I don't see why,' said Frances truthfully. 'I feel no chagrin.'

'You may not, but he does. And not just because they have got themselves wed but that they did it in spite of his protest. They'd never have dared had he been king. I think he made the worst choice in refusing the crown.'

Frances could not agree, knowing that she would not have had Robert. But she said nothing.

Within days Mary was regaling her with their father's tenacious pursuit of retribution upon the Duke of Buckingham and his bride.

'He has sent soldiers after them,' Mary informed her joyously.

By the next day she had the full account. 'George Villiers has been forced to flee, and the bride brought back home to her father. And serves her right, the proud tit!'

'Mary!' scolded Frances, but Mary was unrepentant.

'I tell you, Frankie, she'll come here calling on us to intercede for her in begging Papa's mercy. Well I for one will not entertain her, nor will the rest of the family, after the way George Villiers treated you. Papa has vowed he will have him arrested for flaunting his authority. Papa may not be king in name but he still has the power to put him in the Tower for treason.'

In a way, Frances felt sorry for the distraught girl when she came. Had she not been alone in her sympathy she might have gone to her father to beg him to restore Villiers to his bride, but she had her own life to get on with, and nothing must jeopardise her coming marriage.

A double wedding wasn't to be, for all Mary's cajoling. Their father had taken it for granted that his daughters would be wed by the usual civil ceremony with a justice of the peace and a prayer conducted by a chaplain. But

Mary's prospective husband was old-fashioned enough to prefer an Anglican service for his marriage, and in fact insisted on it.

Robert and Frances, having had enough of delay and wary of even more disappointment, were content with whatever mode of service the Lord Protector desired, only too glad of a satisfactory conclusion reached at last with the Earl of Warwick. Besides, Robert had gone down with a fearful cold again some weeks ago, which had left him with a miserable cough that refused to diminish. All he wanted was to have the wedding done with and his wife at his side.

'When we're wed,' he whispered as they lay in their secret nook in Bushey Park, the day unusually warm for October, 'you'll see how quickly this confounded chill will leave me. You are my sweet easement and I praise our dear Lord every hour for His marvellous gift of you.'

She too praised God for this gentle warmth in their joy of each other .

'We'll be so happy, my heart,' she murmured. 'We'll have lots of children – that will make my father proud of us.'

'Perhaps Mary will have more children than you,' he teased, 'and he'll be more proud of her than you.'

'She might not have any,' Frances laughed, but paused in her jest with a feeling that it might be prophetic. There came a passing thought: why hadn't Fauconberg's three years of marriage with his previous wife produced any issue? Hastily she pushed the thought aside. 'But I'm sure she will have,' she added, brightening.

*　　*　　*

Frances wasn't the only one to wonder at Fauconberg's lack of children from his first marriage. A more unscrupulous mind had been dwelling on it, ready to make something witty of it like the court jester he sometimes managed to make himself appear.

His Highness was in his study when Doctor Jeremiah White came to present the following Sunday's sermon for his approval. At his entrance, Oliver stretched his back from his work and beamed up at him, grateful to break from it awhile. He'd always condescended to be on familiar terms with Doctor White, and he grinned at him as the draft sermon was laid before him.

'And how go things with you and your good wife, my dear Jerry?' he enquired convivially.

Jerry grinned. 'So well that she presents a full stomach, and I confess I cannot blame over-indulgence at table.'

'In bed, then?' came the wicked chuckle.

'Indeed, sir.'

'She satisfies you well, then?'

'I could not be more satisfied – nightly!' quipped Jerry.

Still chuckling, and glad to have someone who could turn his mind from the constant fret of his office, Cromwell gazed up at his hovering chaplain.

'You know my youngest daughter Frances is to marry the grandson of the Earl of Warwick, Mr Robert Rich?'

'That I do, and wish her *luck* in her marriage.'

Oliver frowned at the pronounced emphasis on the word 'luck'. 'How so?'

'I hear he is not a robust man, sir, and one's eyes can well bear that out. He has a flushed look about him. But perhaps it is merely from the joy of his coming marriage to your sweet daughter. By your leave, sir, she is pretty enough to cause the whitest snowdrop to grow rosy at her touch.'

Oliver had relaxed again. 'You are a rogue!' he laughed, but again grew serious. 'You know the Viscount Fauconberg?'

Jerry folded his arms loosely, at ease and prepared for half an hour at least in his master's office. 'Perfectly well,' he replied.

'I am going to marry my daughter Mary to him. What do you think of the matter?'

'I think, sir,' Jerry said slowly, 'why, I think he will never make Your Highness a grandfather.'

'I'm sorry to hear that, Jerry,' returned Oliver, his camaraderie with his young chaplain such that the man's audacity had not ruffled him in the slightest. 'How do you know?'

Jerry had become suddenly serious. He leaned towards his master a little. 'I speak in confidence, Your Highness. There are certain defects in Lord Fauconberg that will always prevent him making you a grandparent, let him do what he can.'

For a moment the other's face clouded, but the next instant he broke into another hearty laugh as though viewing a joke. 'Well, they are to wed, and I think it will be best for them to settle the account of defects as best they can. I'm sure you must be mistaken.'

It was Jerry's cue to laugh now. 'I'm sure I must be,' he quipped lightly and, excusing himself while His Highness was still in a high mood, left the room.

*   *   *

Betty's new baby had been born within a week of the inauguration of his grandfather as Lord Protector, having refused the title of king. She'd called him Oliver in his honour, and it was a delight to see how her father had become so taken with the boy.

'He will go on to great things,' he announced firmly, holding him in his arms in that awkward, overprotective manner of a man uncertain of his own strength and that of the child he holds.

'And now I have three sons as well as a daughter,' Betty stated, proud of her achievement in the face of those continuing stomach pains of hers. 'I thank God for giving me such good fortune.'

'How can she give thanks for her *good fortune*,' Mary cynically observed, 'when all she ever seems to have is misfortune in regard to her health?'

While at three months, little Oliver was proving to be a healthy enough child, Betty appeared to be taking an inordinate length of time to regain her strength. Unable to feed him, she had found a wet nurse, and although Betty made herself join the family in their daytime apartments, she often looked as though she'd be far better staying in bed.

'I can't see her going back to Norborough,' said Frances. 'I think she'll be staying here permanently. The bother is that this family is growing by leaps and bounds. Very soon it will outgrow even Whitehall.'

Her brother Richard, soon to become a member of the Privy Council, also spent much time here in his splendid apartments, enjoying his title of Lord Richard. With him were Doll and their three children: the oldest, Beth; little Dorothy, now two years old; and the baby born last year – a boy, to Richard's great joy, another Oliver. And Doll was again pregnant.

Bridget and Charles Fleetwood with their army of children visited often now that her father had 'regained his soul', as Bridget put it, by his refusal of the crown. She had fiercely opposed any idea of his becoming king – to her it would have been a blasphemy, she and Charles being both Republicans and strongly Baptist.

Fauconberg too had rooms in the palace, his seat in the new House of Peers demanding he be nearby, which of course delighted Mary.

The evenings became merrier as the weddings approached. His Highness, mostly at the centre of the crowded gatherings, was more relaxed than Frances had seen him in a long time, calling for music – which he loved – and endlessly twitting everyone and playing jokes on them.

'He's like the father we knew as children,' she said to Mary. 'He even had Betty laughing. I think she is beginning to rally at last. I only wish Papa would be less distant towards my darling Robert. He tends to hold him at arm's length, whereas he always appears at ease with your Thomas, always bantering with him.

Mary gave her a sympathetic look. 'Papa's skylarking can become a little excessive at times, as you well know, and your Robert doesn't always look up to returning like for like, even as a joke.'

Mary was right. Robert did appear flushed of cheek lately, as if he had a perpetual fever, though he assured her he felt quite well.

'I've always had a high colour,' he said.

'Not when I first met you,' she returned, but he laughed.

'It was from fear of being spurned by you, I being so in love with you.'

Oliver did feel much more at ease with Fauconberg than ever he did with his youngest daughter's fiancé, enjoying nothing more than exchanging jibes with a man who could give back as good as he got, who did not shrink from his sort of wit or even from a little horseplay at times. Robert wasn't given to it at all, while Fauconberg was, being a man of remarkably quick mind and stamina.

It was always good when the women retired to bed, leaving the men to themselves. With Fauconberg, Rich, Claypole, Dick and sometimes Fleetwood – he often wished Henry were with them too – they'd drink late into the night, enjoying small talk, poking fun at the two prospective husbands, with Fauconberg taking it all in good part while Rich sometimes looked lost, even though he'd smile good-naturedly.

It was that man's mounting nervousness of the approaching event that was usually the butt of jest from Dick, who, as an old friend, was well at ease with him. Fauconberg, however, seemed quite bereft of nerves.

'I wonder you can contain y'self these next weeks,' slurred Oliver, draining his fifth glass of sherry sack, without his wife to carp at him for his over-indulgence.

'I contain myself as best I can,' answered Thomas, laughing.

'You hide your impatience very well,' put in Richard. 'I say that for you.'

'Oh, I am impatient,' returned Thomas, 'but I contain it well.'

'Which is more than could ever be said of Dick,'

chuckled his father, looking blearily at his son. 'Never have I seen a man so lost in nerves, and so dressed like a peacock that none could've missed him. He shone, man! My God, he shone!'

John Claypole was regarding Fauconberg, his head tilted slightly, his somewhat full face bright with appraisal. 'I c'n quite imagine your patience, my dear Thomas. Commendable patience 'n' fortitude.'

Fauconberg gazed back at him, his eyes narrowing. 'I've had practice, my dear Claypole. To lose a wife yet retain one's composure without breaking down like a fool – that calls for a deal of patience and fortitude. I pray you never know.'

Seeing things becoming sombre, Oliver made his tone jocular and vociferous. 'When you and your new wife have two or three brats wrangling around your feet, Thomas, then talk you of patience and fortitude. Then will you need all the patience you can lay your hands on.'

'Sir?' queried Fauconberg, frowning.

'Not brats then,' chaffed Oliver. 'Your pardon, my dear Tom. Though whichever word you call them by, should you have any at all, they'll still seem as vexing. Then I say will your patience be tried to the limit.'

Seeing the bewildered smile, Oliver guessed he'd somehow lost him along the way and made an effort to bring him back on course again.

'Unless you intend to do me out of the joy of being grandparent. Though having suffered a lifetime of children,I wonder sometimes if it might not be wiser to abstain from mewling babes and live tranquil and unencumbered. Ah, who can tell? But that one might fall prey to those who would jest that one might not be capable of the begetting.' With this joke he leaned over sideways, laughing. But though Thomas still half smiled, it had become fixed.

'Who says that?'

'Why, my own chaplain, Doctor White. But then he is a man for the joke and his words are of no consequence.'

'Then I shall take them as the normal prating of a clown,' said Fauconberg, his tone light, though the smile remaining forced, while the general conversation passed away from him on to others.

With some measure of surprise and a deal of pleasure, Doctor Jeremiah White read the letter handed to him by a messenger the next morning. It was from Viscount Fauconberg, desiring his company. His first thought was that he might well be required to officiate at the coming marriage, though surely a minister more exalted than he would have been selected. Filled with curiosity, he made his way through Whitehall to the Viscount's study at the appointed time; the door was opened by the Viscount himself, hardly had he tapped on it.

'Ah, Doctor White, my good fellow, come in!'

The first thing White noticed was that for a young man his face bore a grave look, almost austere, yet it was friendly enough. The face was strongly handsome, although the man himself was only of medium height.

Fauconberg stood back for Jerry to enter, closing the door after him and deftly turning the key in the lock. It was then he noticed how tight Fauconberg's face had become. He noticed too for the first time that the man carried a stout cane.

'Now, my dear Doctor White, what foul lies have you been saying to my prospective father-in-law?'

White eyed the cane, feeling a coldness creep across his cheeks. Already preparing to defend himself should it be raised at him, he smiled as cheerily as he could, hoping his face did not look as sick as he felt.

'I truly do not know what you are referring to, my lord,' he managed.

The tight features were beginning to become mottled with anger. 'You foul rascal! How dare you tell such mischievous lies of me as you have to the Protector!'

'I don't know what lies you speak of.'

'That I could never make him a grandfather,' enlightened Fauconberg, stepping forward in growing rage. 'I shall break every bone in your damned body, you troublesome, devil-ridden scoundrel!'

Prepared to deflect the first swipe, White was still caught out by his assailant's energetic leap forward, the cane coming down painfully across his shoulders.

'What d'you say for yourself, hey?' bellowed Fauconberg, the stick ascending again and again, with Jeremiah White trying desperately to catch at it before being finally forced to protect his head while Fauconberg continued to bellow, 'What excuse can you make? What excuse?'

Between the blows, White managed to shriek, 'My lord – leave me be! My lord – let me explain.'

The cane was lowered. 'Explain then.'

But the danger hadn't passed, threatening to burst out again at any second. Jerry spoke fast, rubbing his now bruised arms.

'My lord, you're too angry for me to hope for

84

mercy, but surely you cannot be too angry to forget justice. You've only to prove me wrong by begetting a child.'

'What?' The cane was being raised.

White gabbled on as fast as he could. 'Should you prove me wrong, then inflict your punishment with just deserve and I'll gladly bear it. If you must exercise your cane, lay it about my Lord Protector's shoulders for betraying but a passing remark of mine.'

Fauconberg's chuckle wasn't a friendly one. 'By God, you have a fine nerve, sir! And by God, sir, I shall do my damnedest to prove you wrong.'

Without another word he turned and unlocked the door, moving aside to allow White to vacate the room as quickly as the swollen weals on his back, shoulders, neck and cheeks would let him.

Preparations for the approaching marriages were becoming daily more agitated. In her room, Frances was having creams smoothed into her hands and face by Marie. It didn't matter that the last days of October were already looking more like winter, with hoar frost riming the almost bare trees and mists hanging about until gone midday, and the sun hardly having time to struggle through before being shrouded again by early afternoon. In her heart it was still summer.

'Seven days remaining, Marie,' she breathed excitedly for the tenth time that morning. Each time she said it, her stomach churned with joy and nerves. Yet, in the midst of it all, Robert's health worried her.

'He seems well enough in spirits, even elated. If only he didn't look so – how can I put it? – delicate. That's the only way to describe it. As though he might break, like a brittle leaf. And his colour is so high. It can't be natural, Marie.'

'What does 'is doctor say, dame?'

'That he is susceptible to summer chills, but it should abate with the colder weather. But it is already cold and he still looks too flushed for my peace of mind. It looks to be a perpetual fever, but that it doesn't appear to trouble him as a true fever might.'

Marie concentrated on massaging cream into her mistress's fingers. 'As you say, dame, 'e remains well in 'is spirits, no? So it cannot be so serious.'

'Perhaps you are right, Marie. Perhaps I am worrying needlessly.'

'Oui, per'aps so,' Marie murmured comfortingly as she continued to gently knead the fingers while Frances, thus lulled, pushed her worries aside.

For all the fretting and counting the days, when the day finally arrived, it hardly seemed like a marriage ceremony at all, taking place on a Thursday, the eleventh of November. She and Robert met in a simple room with a simple table, to be joined together by a justice of the peace, followed by a short prayer from one of Papa's chaplains for their future happiness and continuing love of God.

With family and friends offering congratulations, Frances could only feel stunned by the brevity of it all. She didn't feel at all married. It was only later that it came to her, as, in a brief moment of respite, Robert stole a kiss and murmured against her cheek, 'My wife, my own loving wife.' Then she knew that no one could ever tear them apart, and all she wanted was to be alone with him to let the significance of those words sink into her. But that had to wait awhile.

The ceremony had been brief as the festivities at Whitehall afterwards were long. Going on until first light, the music was supplied by forty-eight violins and as many trumpets, with mixed dancing to scandalise the more Puritan-hearted when later the broadsheets reported it. Meantime her father showed no care to what the world thought of him as he frolicked with the guests, cajoling them to join in the dancing while he sang at the top of his tuneless voice despite disapproving glances from his wife.

'Our guests are here to see the happy couple,' he insisted when Frances held back, seeing how weary Robert looked. 'We cannot disappoint them.'

Even Betty, who'd pushed herself to attend, despite gnawing stomach pains, was urged time and again to display the old energy she once had.

'As much as I'm glad to see Papa in such high spirits,' she said to her mother, 'I'd be less embarrassed were he to try to control them.' And to her mother's concurring nod, went on, 'He has put several ladies to some disarray by throwing sherry sack over their dresses, though they are too polite to reproach him. I saw him a little while ago putting wet sweetmeats on their chair seats.' And to Frances a warning: 'Look carefully before you sit on any seat, Frankie.'

Mary's wedding, held at Hampton Court, was a far quieter affair, at Thomas' insistence. At his insistence too, and although they were first joined in a civil ceremony, there was a second service conducted by the Anglican Doctor Hewitt from the Book of Common Prayer in the traditional style that only a few years ago the Cromwell of old would have frowned upon.

'I will have our marriage solemnised in the proper sight of God,' he told Mary privately.

Also in contrast to Frances' lavish wedding feast, Mary's was a quiet celebration, with the minimum of music provided for a pastoral or two by Andrew Marvell, in which the guests themselves took part, her father playing a definitely non-singing part out of deference to the rest, and possibly because he had tired himself out by the previous cavorting only a week ago.

For Frances and Robert, peace had come at last. Not that he had much energy left in him to do more than sleep beside her. He was tender with her, but it was the tenderness of a man bereft of vitality. She could not truthfully say that he made love to her in the true sense of the word. He'd kiss her, fondle her, and she, rising to the urgency, would find him half risen and having to apologise for his failing, saying that he must be overtired and that if he rested awhile he would be ready for her.

She was so in love with her gentle, sweet husband that she was only too willing for him to rest, while, partly hurt, partly concerned, she lay miserably awake listening to his soft breathing and telling herself that after a while he'd awake to complete his lovemaking, or that tomorrow night would see her fulfilled. But it was the same story, and as the days and weeks progressed it did not improve. Christmas came and went and still her marriage remained unconsummated. Yet he did love her – that she knew.

Seven

Oliver regarded his physician closely. 'Are you certain?'

'Most certainly, Your Highness – the king's evil, most certainly. The painfulness and swelling of the joints and the swelling of the glands in the neck all point to it. I have examined him most closely, and, with regret, that is my firm diagnosis. There is little else I can do but administer potions that will ease the pains of the joints.'

Oliver's eyes didn't leave the other's face, which was as bleak as the bitter winter weather beyond the study window. 'Is his wife aware?'

'I do not think she yet realises the full portent of it.'

'Then I would prefer she is not untimely enlightened.'

The physician looked troubled. 'She should be warned, sir.'

'I think not.'

'To prepare her . . .'

'I would have her left in blessed ignorance for the while.'

With this, Oliver terminated the consultation in his usual fashion by politely but firmly showing the man from the room.

*   *   *

Some said it was the coldest winter in living memory. Frances sat by the fire with Robert opposite, his aching limbs held off the wooden armrests of his chair by soft pillows.

She let her gaze wander from the bible on her lap to the midday weather outside, thankful that she didn't have to venture out there, where the snow in places came up to a man's knees. Where the wind had blown it, there were drifts deep enough to easily cover a horse and coach, and when the wind did decide to drop and the sky to clear, frost held everything in an iron grip.

Since Christmas, they had remained in their apartments in Whitehall, where they had moved to from Warwick House because of Robert's decline in health, safe from the bitter weather while she nursed him, read to him, her only joy to be his companion until this chill of his departed.

'I'm being a burden to you,' he murmured, seeing her gaze wander to the window.

She turned quickly back to him, and in case he had misread her thoughts, gave him a reassuring smile. 'My dearest, you are not. I'm most content. Nothing would induce me to venture out into that terrible weather. We're safe and warm here and can curl up in our own little haven together – two closeted little dormice – until the spring awakens us.'

He smiled wanly at her allegory. 'And should these aching joints still keep me confined indoors once the weather breaks, will you then be so content to stay closeted with this weakling husband of yours? I hate to see you so pensive.'

Putting aside the bible she'd been reading aloud to

him, Frances rose and came to drop a fond kiss on his brow. 'You will be quite recovered by then. We'll put this dreadful weather behind us when the sun returns in all its warmth. We'll go gathering spring flowers together and you can present me with a pretty posy.'

He raised his face to hers, returning her kiss. 'I pray it be so, but there are times—'

'Not another doleful word.' She placed a tender, loving finger to his lips. 'I'll not have you speak so.'

Holding him close to her, feeling the weakness with which he let his head fall on her bosom, she continued, 'With the going of this cold weather, these aches and pains will all disappear. Doctor Goddard will soon have you well again. He is a clever physician and he is satisfied with your progress.'

'Did he tell you that?' asked Robert with new hope.

'He had no need. His confident manner when he speaks to me of you says all. And now . . .' Going back to her chair, she retrieved the bible to open it again on her lap. 'I shall read on until you tire and need me to stop.'

He loved listening to the scriptures. They seemed to comfort him. He'd have read for himself but that his hands would begin to ache from holding a book, even a smaller one, for any length of time – and anyway she was only too happy to while away the long hours by reading aloud, she too gaining comfort, not only from the holy words but from Robert's expression of peace as he listened.

'And we are fortunate to have so many loving people about us,' she added before starting to read again. 'Not a day passes without some member of the family coming to see how you do. Indeed, my love, so many visit us that I hardly have enough hours in the day, so much occupies me. I certainly have no time to be pensive, as you put it.'

She did have plenty to occupy her. Papa came as often as his duties allowed; her mother too. Dick visited regularly with Dorothy, to playfully chide Robert for his malingering.

But she missed Mary. Having taken up residence with her husband at Fauconberg House in Soho Street, Mary was so happy there that she seldom thought to visit Whitehall. Frances felt her absence strongly. She missed the old days when they would share secrets, giggle together – she even missed their petty squabbles.

Betty came to pay a visit after Robert had retired to his room for a nap. Dear Betty, trying so hard to put her own ill health aside.

'You are too pale, Frankie,' she remarked and, eyeing the drab brown dress, its skirts limp from days of wearing, she added, 'Is there nothing else to wear but that?'

'I go nowhere these days,' returned Frances, 'to need many changes of dress.'

'You are becoming a recluse.' She wrinkled her nose against the close air of the room. 'You're still a young woman, yet here you are shut away from the world and behaving like some middle-aged hag, even to dressing so. I'll have you a bright new dress made.'

'I have bright dresses. Would you have me prance about here in frills and ribbons?'

Betty wasn't listening. 'We'll venture out together and spend a day with my dressmaker. Robert will be safe left in Doctor Goddard's hands.'

'I'd rather not,' said Frances firmly.

'Then I shall visit her alone and bid her make you something pretty.'

Within a week there arrived a velvet-covered box containing a gown of rich cerise velvet with an underskirt of pearly satin. The frills at the cuffs and along the low décolletage were swathed in the same pearly satin, with little rosettes of cerise velvet; the bodice and hem were embroidered in gold.

'But I've a wardrobe of such gowns,' protested Frances to Robert as she lifted the lid of the box. 'Betty cannot think us poverty-stricken as well as being, as she puts it, reclusive.' But she thanked her graciously for all that. Not for all the world would she have wanted to spoil Betty's good if somewhat misguided intentions.

Unfortunately, before a day could be arranged for her to parade herself in her dress before her loving and generous sister, Betty again fell victim to her stomach pains, and although Frances felt sorry for her, she couldn't help feeling thankful that she hadn't been obliged to leave Robert's side to go off flaunting Betty's gift before her. He was so unwell that she felt he needed her by him constantly.

John Thurloe, working in his office after most had gone to bed, was disturbed by a gentle knock at his door. He frowned towards the table clock – a quarter of the hour past eleven.

'Come!' he ordered irritably.

The man, who entered somewhat breathlessly and who Thurloe recognised as an obscure member of the House, held a letter out to him.

'Forgive the intrusion at this hour, sir, but the matter is of the utmost importance. This letter is for His

Highness's urgent attention, and strongly recommends he goes down to the House in the morning first thing – to do service for the Army and for the nation.'

A knowing looked passed from the man to Thurloe. The Republican Members in Parliament had been agitating to destroy the new Constitution for some time, and, with no love for the new Upper Chamber, were keen only for the return of the Rump Parliament. For a long while, Cromwell had been watching the proceedings in the Commons with growing anger, and now it seemed his anger was justified.

Cromwell was in bed; that Thurloe knew. He went to John Maidstone, Cromwell's most treasured valet, but found him reluctant to disturb him.

'Can it not wait until morning?' he demurred.

'Wake him up, man!' thundered Thurloe, pushing him down the corridor to Cromwell's bedchamber. 'This is an affair of state, and cannot wait.'

Uncertainly, Maidstone tapped on the door. 'Knock, sir! Knock hard. Harder!' roared Thurloe.

Maidstone did as he was told until they heard a muffled but peeved voice demanding who was there.

Thurloe stated his business, and in a few moments the door opened. His face lined and blotched from being so rudely awakened, Cromwell's once penetrating grey eyes were watery and red-veined. But on reading the letter, sleep dropped from him – he was once more the alert statesman.

He spent the rest of the night in preparation to foil the troublesome Republicans, dispatching his brother-in-law Desborough and his cousin Whalley to change the guard, for security's sake.

The next morning – an icy February one – he was

up early, and at nine o'clock was already bolting down his dinner in eagerness to be at the House, knowing he could be there all day without another meal inside him.

Frances met him in a passageway, her face white and strained from lack of sleep, her hair not brushed, her dress merely flung on in her haste to find help, her maid hurrying behind her.

'Papa!' Her cry on seeing him was one of relief. 'I'm so glad to find you. My poor Robert – I fear for him. Would you summon Doctor—'

'Not now!' he bellowed, almost pushing her aside in his haste. Before she could say any more he had rushed on, making for the rear of the palace and the river steps.

The air struck him keen as a sword blade as he emerged from Whitehall, but he hardly noticed until at the steps to the water's edge he was greeted by a river frozen solid, his boatman poking at the ice with a pole, at a loss how to get his master to Westminster.

But Cromwell solved the problem for him. With an impatient 'Pah!' and a rounded curse, he turned and hurried back to the palace. Reaching the mews, he clambered up into the driving seat of a coach being prepared to take some envoy to some part of the City, and, brushing aside his coachman's protest that it only had two horses so far, he drove off like a fury in the direction of Westminster. His anger, which he'd kept in fine control until faced with the immutable barrier of a frozen Thames, exploded in a rage as the careering, depleted team seemed not half fast enough.

'What friends do I have?' he yelled at empty air.

'None, as I see! They put me down at every turn, argue even the toss of a coin with me.'

Blind to the stares of Londoners going about their ordinary Friday morning business, astonished at the spectacle of the Lord Protector driving like a madman through the streets with his mounted bodyguard trying to catch up with him, Cromwell's mind seethed with all the burdens that fell upon him. Men plotting against him at every turn, willing to pull down the country for their selfish aims – the Sealed Knot for one.

Thurloe had managed to keep them disrupted through one of their own Members, an informant named Sir Richard Willys. The Royalist Ormonde, who Cromwell had defeated at Drogheda, had arrived heavily disguised, but little escaped Thurloe's spies, and Cromwell had been alerted. But to have him arrested and tried for treason wouldn't have enhanced Cromwell's reputation for fair-mindedness, so he'd arranged for Lord Broghill to frighten him into fleeing the country.

Problems didn't stem only from his enemies, but often from those so close to him that he could hardly believe it. From Henry came constant beleaguering over lack of money sent to pay debts accrued in Ireland.

'Why?' he barked at astonished faces as he drove past. 'Why do I have such trouble with my own son, whom I've lovingly made Commander-in-Chief over that whole damned country?' He never had the same carping from General Monck, who had equal command of Scotland. Then there was Fleetwood, being driven on by Bridget to question his every decision. And now was this latest escapade from Parliament.

By the time he reached the House, his temper was so foul that he had to compose himself in a retiring room with a mug of ale and some toast to ease the stabbing pains from the stone in his insides before continuing into the Chamber. Even here a warbling Fleetwood accosted him, begging him to desist from his obvious intent.

'Think, sir, what you are about to do.'

'Think?' Oliver roared at him. 'I shall tell you what I think. You are a milksop! By the living God, I will dissolve the House!'

Throwing down the remains of the toast, he strode past Fleetwood towards the Commons Chamber to deliver his speech of dissolution.

In the Commons they listened like chastised pupils while he stormed at them, reminding them that it was they who had granted that he name another House and that with integrity he had named it:

> . . . out of men that can meet you wheresoever you go, and shake hands with you and tell you it is not titles, it is not lordship, it is not this or that which they value but a Christian and English interest – men of your own rank and quality and men that I approved my heart to God in choosing, men that I hoped would not only be a balance to a Common's House of Parliament but to themselves, having honest hearts, loving the same things as you love, whilst you love England and whilst you love religion.

In silence they sat while in his usual manner Cromwell strung out his speech, going on far longer than need be, with dramatic warnings of Charles Stuart being poised at the very water's edge to invade, and England in danger of being plunged once again into bloodshed and confusion because of their own incompetence as a Parliament.

'If this, I say, be the effect of your sitting, I think it is high time an end be put to your sitting, and I do declare to you here that I do dissolve this Parliament. Let God judge between you and me.'

His speech finally ending, there came a defiant chorus of 'Amen' from the Republicans.

Sitting by Robert's bed, Frances felt she would never be able to forgive her father. When she most needed him, he'd thrust her aside, leaving her to cope with her poor husband, who she was now certain hadn't much longer to live.

All that night Robert had tossed and turned in pain from the swelling in his neck and infected joints. All Doctor Goddard could do was administer laudanum.

She'd clung to hope that morning. If he had the king's evil, as Doctor Goddard finally told her he had, a king's touch would cure him. But England had no king. Yet Papa had been urged time and time again to take up the kingship – had he done so he would now be God's anointed. He'd come as near to being king as any ordinary man could. Her only remaining hope – perhaps foolish, but she'd been desperate – had been that had Papa come at her bidding with an earnest prayer for God to be in his fingertips as he laid hands on her poor husband, surely God would have healed through a man who'd selflessly deemed himself to be unworthy to become his anointed.

But her father had thrust her aside and hurried off to his troublesome Parliament instead. She now sensed that the miracle would not happen, that her father's hands would be merely those of a man. In ignoring her plea for help, he had lost God's help too.

For days she had been sitting by Robert's bedside, watching him grow weaker. Her father came, but she was stiff with him, and when he cuddled her close in his sorrow for her, she couldn't respond. He didn't know, didn't realise. He took her attitude for grief and went sadly away.

He too was sick. The ague he'd picked up from the Irish bogs had always bothered him, and of late had become so frequent and vicious that he also had to take to his bed, sweating and groaning. Coupled with the stone and bouts of gout, ill health was slowly wearing him down.

Valiantly he struggled on. Two days after Parliament's dissolution he entertained his officers at the Cockpit opposite Whitehall, trying to create an atmosphere of friendliness while they declared loyalty. But Frances learned from her mother how he had expressed doubts of those loyalties lasting longer than the wine in their stomachs.

Nor was he well when, one week later, Doctor Goddard announced that Frances should send for her and Robert's families to hasten to the bedside, an announcement that sent a chill through her body as she complied. Ill or not, her father came, looking more as though it should be him on his deathbed rather than Robert, whose cheeks were so flushed with chronic fever as to make a farce of his condition. His breath, however, came so rapid that it seemed not to have enough energy in it to keep him alive.

There was no gratitude in her heart for her father's presence as she prayed on her knees for Robert's life.

She even found herself wishing her father could be made to take her dear husband's place. Her father was old and done with the world. Robert was still young, with too much to live for to bid it farewell.

An hour later, collapsed in inconsolable grief over that finally stilled body, she flinched from her father's touch on her shoulder in his effort to comfort her. It should have been him lying there and Robert's hands touching her.

But her beloved's hands would never again do that, his arms never again hold her close, and she felt nothing but hatred towards the one who might have saved her dearest, most loved one but for his greater love of politics and self-esteem.

The funeral took place on the twenty-ninth of February, a bitterly cold Friday, the route through the City lined with silent crowds sorrowing for the young widow. Before being conducted to the family vault at Felstead, Robert's remains had lain in state for three days at Warwick House, draped in purple like a prince.

A prince. Frances thought of that with bitterness – a great funeral being ordered by her father, when he could have saved that life. It was too late now to make amends by all this needless pomp and circumstance.

She sat in the leading coach of the long cortège, her strained, white face shielded from public gaze behind a thick, black silk veil. She had sat so long holding Robert's hand as illness drained his life away that it was as though she had become part of him, that when his end came she too would die, Death travelling from his body to hers as a single entity. But it wasn't to be. They had released her hand gently from his, separating them forever, he to go to glory, she to continue on in this world. She had tried to cling on, had cried out in protest, but they had been insistent, and now this part of him, prised from his dead body and forced to continue living in her without its soul, was a mere shell, quite empty.

Her prince. Twenty-three years old, the eager young gallant she had striven so long to have for her husband – who had loved her with such tenderness that at times she could hardly speak for the joy of him, who had laughed with her, teased her, made gentle love to her – had in three short months of their marriage been reduced to a shadow. She had watched his life drain away, watched Death – eager for his plunder – come to claim him, watched him pluck out that last shuddering breath from her dear beloved to leave her utterly destroyed.

'I have nothing,' she whispered to her mother, her voice hardly heard through the veil, and her mother's arm came around her shoulders in an effort to draw the pain out from her youngest daughter and into her own body, while her father sat with head bent, silent in his sorrow for her – as well he might.

Eight

The terrible grip of winter 1657 suddenly gave way in March 1658 to warm balmy breezes.

Released from the bitter cold, England went about its daily life with the languor of a man having eaten a heavy meal after a long fast. Oliver too appeared to the country to be sufficiently recovered to continue his duties as though they'd never been interrupted.

The dissolution of Parliament had left him free to concentrate on his foreign policies, which he did with a ferocious energy that often surprised his followers and alarmed his enemies, who saw him as practically indestructible, having survived all plots against his life, illnesses, uprisings and personal grief.

Yet there was something amiss in him.

'I feel the reins slipping from me with every passing day,' he said to his wife in May.

'How can that be?' she queried, ever a pillar to him through his low spirits. 'Your reputation in the world has never been so high. You have able commanders in both Ireland and Scotland, with George Monck and our own dear Henry both so well respected.'

But today his spirits remained low. 'Nine years since I took up the reins. My only friend these days is George Monck. In London I have just my dear Thurloe, my

103

shrewd and inventive statesman, as loyal and trusted as my own right arm.'

Elizabeth clicked her tongue. 'You cannot be so forsaken as to have just two friends in the world. What of your loving family?'

'Loving family,' he repeated morosely while gazing into the empty grate, the warmer weather needing no fire to be lit. 'Bridget is as stiff a Republican as ever there was, sour as vinegar and as cold towards me as was this very winter, her husband Fleetwood incapable of making up his mind without report to her. My poor Frances I cannot bestow any manner of comfort upon, who pushes me from her in her grief for her dead husband.'

Angrily he brushed away the threatening moisture from his eyes. He'd always been an emotional man, but he wept too easily of late, like one in his second childhood. Indeed he'd heard that Henry had written to Lord Broghill wishing his father were equally distant from both his childhoods!

'As for the others,' he continued hastily, 'my own cousin Whalley and my sister's husband Desborough join with half my officers in decrying me for royal pretentiousness in speaking of Christ's return and accusing me of usurping His throne. I'm estranged from those who were once my friends – Henry Vane and Thomas Harrison now in Carrisbrooke for their sins – but who now accuse me of betraying the cause of righteousness. Ludlow, Goffe, Lambert – all of them against me.'

'You've had men against you all your life,' Elizabeth said gently. 'But you have always triumphed over them and will do so again.' She'd always believed in him, but he seldom noticed. He did not notice now.

'I've not the strength any more. I'm beset by dissention. Even my own dear Betty lobbies me, crying to me to prevent the execution of Doctor Hewitt and Sir Henry Slingsby. She will not see that men who go preaching and plotting against government must reap charges of treason. Mary and her husband are petitioning Cardinal Mazarin to intervene for Slingsby. He may be related to Fauconberg by marriage, but he is a Royalist agitator and indeed took part in the Penruddock uprising for which he was once imprisoned. But that is not Fauconberg's fault.'

He gave her an apologetic smile. 'I do try you so, my dear Joan. You are my truest friend, and I should thank God for you rather than cry to you with my woes, but there are times I weary of it all.'

'I know, dear, I know.' Rising, she put down the embroidery she'd let fall idle when Oliver came into the room, and came over to pat the heavily veined hand lying loosely on the armrest. The smile she gave him was full of encouragement, though it disguised her own feelings of desolation as to where her family appeared to be heading.

Wealthy they were, beyond dreams, the Cromwell name renowned from Russia to the New World. To think that as an obscure country gentleman and mere Member of Parliament for Cambridge, he had at one time almost emigrated to America. Now he was a power in the world, and all of Europe looked to him. In the continuing hostilities with Spain, he'd promised to aid France by sending a fleet to Spanish-held Flanders, his reward to be the port of Dunkirk. Yet all this wealth, this power, was an empty cask as death and ill health stalked the family.

Frankie's loss had been deeply felt, she still so young, without even the hope of a child to comfort her. Betty was hardly ever well for two days at a time, though she bore her burden bravely. Then there was Oliver himself – she sometimes felt the icy touch of death about him. Was it the burden of his office, or merely advancing years that made him victim to so many diverse afflictions? He strove so hard to show to the world the picture of a man still strong and able, but in the bosom of his family he was a different person.

'Forgive me my absence,' he'd say after several days confined to his room. 'I've been troubled by a migraine and giddiness,' or, 'A most painful pustule on my back had to be drawn.' There were reports of him swooning, and there were still the recurrent fevers of ague, and always the problem of the kidney stones he'd so long endured. He may present a fine face to the world, but she shuddered, as, patting his hand, she contemplated the future with secret dread.

Family supper at Hampton Court was usually taken in privacy in her mother's suite of rooms, unless her father had specific guests, when he would entertain them elsewhere. This evening, to Frances' relief, the family was all together.

It was June. The rays of a setting sun struck through the windows, but the room was still uncomfortably warm, despite them being wide open. Summer was proving the hottest in years, just as winter had proved the coldest. London stank of refuse, attracting clouds of flies, and the putrid air of the City hung like a mist over everything.

Here the country felt cleaner. Papa was spending a

week at a time at his beloved Hampton Court, his health no longer up to weekend travel, and plague being an ever-present concern in the City in summer, so those needing audience with the Lord Protector must travel from London on Tuesdays and Thursdays.

For Frances the palace was no longer beautiful or carefree, wherever she went her thoughts recalling the time she'd spent here with Robert. No longer did she ride out to Bushey Park, for the paths she would have to follow would be those they had once followed. Even to think of their secret place was as a knife piercing her heart, knowing that the same slender saplings still grew there, the ivy leaves still scrambling through them, the same soft, mossy floor, unchanging, continuing, while Robert was gone forever. Their very continuation struck her as cruel mockery.

She had even come near to requesting that the saplings be felled, the ivy cleared away, but when it came to it she could not have it done, as if Robert would cry out in agony of that part of him being severed.

In grief she told her mother how she felt, Mama doing her best to comfort her. Everyone was so supportive, trying to do what they could to lessen her pain – her own immediate family and her aunts, Jane Desborough and the sweet Robina Wilkins, who knew what it was to lose a beloved husband, Aunt Catherine also once a widow and even the spinster Aunt Elizabeth.

Henry's twenty-six-year-old brother-in-law, Sir John Russell, also visited her on several occasions, adding his sympathy. He too was very kind and understanding of her grief. He was very like his sister, possessing quiet charm and the noble but agreeable looks of the great Russell family, and though he was of medium height, his upright bearing made him appear taller than he was.

Yet as much as Frances appreciated everyone's efforts, she would rather have been left alone, but had not the heart to hurt them by saying so.

One she keenly missed was Mary, now with her husband in France. Papa had sent him on a good-will visit to King Louis after the capture of Dunkirk, Gravelines and Mardyke from the Spanish. Their first letters had come by Cromwell's private messenger, and this evening the Protectoress quietly claimed her right to read aloud to those gathered around the supper table, an eager hush settling as the letter was broken from its seal and unfolded with an expensive crackling.

Elizabeth cast her eyes quickly over Mary's spidery handwriting, coming to the part that permitted shared listening.

'Our dear Mary writes how marvellously she and her husband were received by both Cardinal Mazarin and His Majesty.' She looked up and smiled towards Oliver. 'We well know how haughty the French King is. Such a fine reception as Mary describes then is in some measure an honour for you, Oliver.'

'The honour is Fauconberg's,' he remarked benevolently, toying with his food.

He ate little these days, his appetite poor. He looked decidedly ill, his florid complexion unhealthily mottled, his eyes rheumy, and when he held his fork – that new invention from Italy now used at table – his hands would tremble.

'I'm told Cardinal Mazarin deems him most agreeable and charming. Did I not say he was the best qualified to take our congratulations to His Majesty, being distantly related to him, so I believe?'

'That you did, dear,' said Elizabeth patiently, and returned to her reading of Mary's letter. 'She says her husband was received with honours more due to a sovereign prince, and that Cardinal Mazarin came to greet him in person as he alighted from his coach.'

'And why not?' interrupted Betty. 'Thomas is no small emissary. He's the Lord Protector's ambassador, and went with a hundred persons to attend his train, bearing letters from you, Papa, and gifts as well. There were two sets of eight English horses for His Majesty, and a set of equally fine horses for His Eminence. Of course he should be treated more as a sovereign prince.'

'And was, my dear,' placated her mother, detecting an argumentative tone, so unlike Betty.

'My letter,' Frances put in with haste as Betty's face, now ravaged by continual pain, grew tight, 'says that the King omitted to wear his crown at his public audience with Thomas, and remained uncovered when his lordship, as Mary calls her husband, made a private visit.'

Her mother's smile was one of gratitude. They'd all seen the change in Betty these past months, her sweet nature being overlaid by tetchiness.

'And the Cardinal, not to be outdone,' Frances rushed on, 'paid a homage to Thomas never before given to an ambassador, coming out of his own apartments, dispensing with public audience, to conduct him into his own cabinet, and afterwards conducting him to the very door of his carriage.'

The tension had decreased, and Frances continued reading her letter to the family. 'Mary says she misses us all and longs to be back here with us, though she admits to enjoying the freedom and laxity of the French court.'

At this Richard burst out laughing. 'I imagine she does! I wager she'll bring back a few outrageous gowns to astound the ladies.'

His arm was still in a splint from a coach accident. He and his father had been attending the launch of a new ship, *The Richard*, when the horses had bolted. The coach had been torn to pieces and he and his father had leapt for their lives. Miraculously, his father was unhurt, but Dick hadn't been so lucky, though it hadn't diminished his sense of humour.

He turned now to Doll. 'I shall have copies of them made for you, my dearest, though they'll have to be somewhat more generous.'

Doll had grown plumper with childbearing, though her fair looks were still with her.

He was about to add to the joke when a footman came hurrying in with a message that Betty was urgently wanted in the nursery. Conversation died as she got up from the table, her expression anxious.

Her father regarded her with equal anxiety. 'Is the little one not well? Why was I not told?'

Little Oliver was the delight of his grandfather, who loved nothing better than dandling him on his knee and hearing him chuckle.

'I expect it's nothing,' replied Betty, dabbing her lips with a napkin as she rose to leave. 'His nurse said he was restless last night. He was a little feverish today when I saw him, but well enough – a little sniffle, nothing more. I shall be back in a moment or two.'

She laid a restraining hand on her husband's arm as he too made to rise. 'Most likely his cold will not let him sleep and he needs his mother.' And she laughed lightly as she went from the room.

It was over so quickly. A fierce fever, nothing could have been done, said the doctors.

Betty's loss of her last-born was awful to witness. She didn't cry, but her eyes stared unseeing, her face white and strained from her grief and her own pains. But when the tiny coffin was lowered from sight some days later, she swooned into her husband's arms and had to be carried to her coach.

Put to bed, she lay for days tossing with the agony of whatever dwelt in her stomach. Doctors solemnly shook their heads, her family realising that all their prayers would be in vain. Thomas and Mary's return home after five days of royal treatment, with presents from the French King and Cardinal Mazarin, was to a household again stricken by the shadow of death.

The royal gifts went unnoticed: a gold box inlaid with diamonds, its value five thousand crowns; a magnificent sword valued at ten thousand crowns; a set of tapestry hangings made in Paris in the Persian style. All this as well as the keys of Dunkirk, presented by the Duke of Crequi, First Lord of the Bedchamber to His Majesty King Louis XIV of France – not a gift but a debt of gratitude – accompanied by the words, 'My Master takes much pleasure in parting with them to the greatest captain on earth.' But it had come too late for the Lord Protector to take any joy from it.

'And so,' he said to his wife as they sat quietly together, 'we have Jamaica in the New World and a stronghold in Europe, yet what have we if we must lose those who are most dear to us?'

*   *   *

'Mall should be here,' snapped Frances as she and her mother came from Betty's suite of rooms, where she lay twisting in physical anguish. 'It's not right that she should go away again at this time.'

'She has a duty to her husband,' her mother excused, but Frances remained angry.

'To go north with him on this tour of Durham at this time points to cruel lack of feeling for us and for Betty.'

'Durham is Fauconberg's home county.' Her mother appeared bent with worry, hands clasped, the fingers hooked against each other in anxiety. 'He has a duty to the people there. It's for a few days. They'll be back soon.'

'Her place is here!' persisted Frances, causing her mother to turn wearily to her.

'Frankie, we have distress enough here. She cannot go against her husband. Her place is with him.'

'Then I blame him for his insensibility,' concluded Frances.

Bridget had come with her family to be here, laying aside differences of opinion with her father. Fleetwood was keeping Henry, who was in Ireland, abreast of all news of his sister. Dick too had taken up residence as Betty's condition rapidly worsened.

'We've done all we can,' Elizabeth told them all. 'Your father hoped that taking the medicinal waters of Tunbridge Wells would help, but the journey appears to have undone the benefits those miraculous waters gave. Doctor Blake diagnosed a large inward swelling in her loins. I have prayed earnestly and hard to the Lord and will continue to do so, and have beseeched the country to join me in this.'

'And so will we all,' declared Bridget fervently. 'The Lord will spare one such as she, the most gentle and charitable of His servants. The Lord will not turn His face from her.'

But all the medicines and potions and prayers proved useless, and the Fauconbergs, who returned at the end of July, saw the worsening situation.'I had no idea she was as ill as this,' whispered Mary to Frances as they sat by their sister's bedside surrounded by the pastel colours she loved best. Pain-racked as she was, her strength ebbing, Betty still managed to receive visitors with that generous spirit that had always characterised her. Propped up on pillows, she smiled at them, her voice but a whisper.

'Thank you all for coming to see me. It cannot be what you would best wish to do on such a lovely day.'

At a loss to know how to reply, Frances lovingly touched the frail hand lying palm upwards on the coverlet like a pale flower.

It was Mary who spoke for her. 'A relief to be out of the heat and in the coolness of these apartments – I've never known such a hot, dry summer as this,' she said brightly. 'Believe it or not, Papa is out hunting with my husband and the Duke of Crequi, who is visiting him.' She was speaking unnaturally fast, her tone too high, too trivial for Frances, as if by it she might dispel the sense that eternal sleep hovered here. 'How they can endure galloping about the countryside in such heat I do not know. I swear he—'

She stopped as Frances caught her arm. Betty's face had creased, her eyelids screwed up before a fearful onslaught of pain. Her cry came in a long, muffled mewling, terrible to hear.

Mary started back in horror, but Frances caught Betty's convulsed hands, squeezing them as hard as she could in hope of killing some of the pain. She turned her face to Mary.

'Summon Doctor Blake, quickly! The opium is wearing off.'

Alone with her sister, Frances clung to those hands, praying, 'Oh, dearest God, in your infinite mercy, take away my darling sister's agony. If you love her, let her dwell in that place where there is no suffering. Dear God, ease her agonies. If you must take her, take her quickly.'

It was sacrilege, praying for death, but what life was left to Betty was but unbearable anguish, and how cruel a God He would be, were He to allow her to suffer longer.

Frances was sure He had heard her. Betty, gasping for breath, now lay in a coma. As hot July moved into even hotter, stifling August, the Quaker George Fox came to Hampton Court. Few knew about it, but Dick let slip to Frances that the man had come and was with Betty at that very moment.

Frances crept into Betty's room to find George Fox sitting by her bed. A broadly built man in his middle thirties, sombrely attired, his hair pulled severely back from his forehead, he glanced towards her as Frances came in, but thereafter ignored her as if she had not been there at all. Daring not to approach any further than the doorway, Frances saw him slowly open the book he held. She heard him begin to read. 'Friend, be still and cool in thy own mind and spirit . . .'

So quiet and deep was his voice, so private the words that Frances stepped back from the chamber, silently closing the door, feeling that she had no right to intrude upon this special moment, personal between him, her sister and God.

Two days later Betty died, quietly, without any sign of those past days of agony, those grim years of pain. In the early hours of the sixth day of August, with her family about her, she smiled with sweet serenity, and, whispering that she felt much better, slipped contentedly into eternal sleep.

Nine

Two weeks since their loss – too early to come to terms with it. For Frances, the merest mention of Betty brought tightness in a throat choked with tears for the emptiness she'd left when she died.

After the funeral, Mary returned to Fauconberg House, laid low by grief. 'I know not what to do with her,' Thomas told Richard. 'She bursts again and again into such weeping that it fairly pulls my heart to pieces.'

It was her father collapsing with a fever that finally brought Mary out of herself enough to come again to Hampton Court to face the place that had witnessed her sister's death, and when he recovered somewhat she'd stayed on. She and Frances sat by an open window overlooking the Fountain Court, the north-facing room giving relief from the afternoon heat.

'I feel ashamed, having shut myself away so. I ought to have thought more on how devastated Papa was by his loss. To collapse as he did was alarming.'

Frances toyed idly with an embroidered handkerchief. 'Betty was his dearest of us all – perhaps because of her frail health for most of her life.' She felt no resentment, just sadness that such a deep love must reap only deeper pain as its reward. 'I fear he may never properly recover from it.'

The day of Betty's death, Papa had to be carried back to his quarters by attendants, his arms about their shoulders, his legs as useless as soft wax. Those hollow, choking sobs had been terrible to hear.

He'd been unable to attend her funeral, so ill had he been, his sister Robina taking the role of chief mourner in his stead. The funeral had taken place at night; the solemn flotilla rowed silently downriver from Hampton Court to Westminster Stairs under a gathering arc of indigo as the last glow of a translucent green horizon faded behind them, as though taking Betty's soul down to rest, for by the time the stairs were reached the glow was gone.

At eleven o'clock her body was borne to the Painted Chamber to rest there until midnight, when it was carried on a stately hearse to the Abbey for interment in the Henry VII Chapel. The procession had been long, with hundreds of courtiers and mourners, but Frances recalled more the absence of her family. Mary and her mother had remained behind to comfort and watch over Papa as he lay in a stupor of grief. Mary's husband had been present, as had Dick, but Dorothy – ten weeks pregnant and suffering continual sickness – had sent her apologies. Bridget and Charles had attended, but Henry had been unable to leave Ireland and had instead written to them all of his profound shock and grief.

'I miss Betty dreadfully,' Mary burst out in a convulsion of weeping that was never very far away, and clapped a linen handkerchief to her eyes. It lay to Frances to put an arm about the quivering shoulders, her own eyes arid as she gazed at the fountain tinkling happily in the shaded court below.

'Please, Mall, you cannot keep distressing yourself so. We all of us need strength to get us through this terrible time.'

She wished she too could cry, but it was as though her tears had all been spent six months before, for her dear Robert, and that empty reservoir hadn't yet refilled enough for her to shed tears for anyone else. Which was worse – to weep until the throat stung and the head throbbed, or to suffer this perpetual aching, like thumping upon an old bruise?

'We must be strong,' Frances repeated adamantly, if only to steel herself. 'Look how Mama is holding us together.'

Her tone must have sounded severe, for Mary quickly wiped her eyes and straightened her back.

'Forgive me, Frankie. I thought it would be she who would have broken down more than Papa, but she is proving to be a stern rock to which we may all cling. I think it is because of her that he is rallying at last.'

Indeed he'd been able to take up some of his duties again, though only at Hampton Court. He had even taken some exercise, riding out to the park.

'The sunshine will do him good,' observed their mother as the fine, hot summer days continued, though with the threat of thundery weather to come. But it was clear that she worried about him.

'I am put out by what I have recently heard,' she said to Bridget when they were alone. 'I am alarmed by some evil remark the Quaker George Fox has made to your father.'

She was sure the man had laid some evil influence

upon Betty and would have had him turned out of the palace had she known of his presence. But recently he had made his presence known again, saying to Oliver as he met him walking in the park that he had seen the waft of death go forth from him. Oliver had been terribly disturbed by it.

'I'm sure he bodes your father ill,' she told Bridget. 'I do not like that man. In fact I am afraid of him.'

'Yield not to unchristian superstition, Mama,' scolded Bridget in her tart manner. 'The Lord will turn away all evil. Do not doubt the Lord.'

The very next day, however, Oliver was again taken unwell, though when she told him of her concern, he managed a sour scoff.

'The man prates too much. It's he who should receive warning – that if he sets himself up too high in this he'll find himself once more in prison for his blasphemies.'

'He frightens me, too,' said Mary as she and Frances wandered in the private garden in late August.

The sun had set but the air was sultry and still, and Frances looked towards the glowing west, noting its ominous haze. 'I wish we could have a storm to clear the air. You shouldn't take notice of such men as George Fox.'

'But he is so deeply religious and preaches such stern love of God.'

Frances gave her a smile. 'Why, Mall, do you intend to join his Society of Friends and go about in black linen?' she quipped to lighten her mood.

But Mary was not having it. 'Of course not!' she snapped and hurried off in a huff leaving Frances smiling after her.

It wasn't often she smiled these days. What was there

to smile about, with Robert gone from her? Grief had matured her. The child she'd been was gone. It seemed to her that she had lived three lives: the first as a silly girl dreaming of love with one who would look like the handsome javelin thrower, Meleager, from the tapestry on the wall of her bedchamber; the second as a married woman, loving and cherishing her husband; now this third life, the widow reflecting on her past. And she was only twenty.

But she was still pretty, and one day must marry again, for a woman alone was a thing to pity, and she would not be pitied by anyone. That thought made her lift her head. Her love for Robert would not bring him back, nor would all the grieving in the world return him to her, nor would he want her to grieve forever, and for all their sakes she must go forward.

Hard-won maturity told her that there were young men who still regarded her with sly admiration – Sir John Russell, for one. If she must remarry one day, he would be as good a choice as any.

This morning he'd visited her father. Papa had complained again of feverishness, and that troublesome Quaker Fox, who had demanded audience with him, had been told he wasn't well enough to receive him. But when John Russell had called, he'd been warmly welcomed, staying more than an hour before Papa's worsening fever forced him to take his leave.

Before going, he had approached Frances as she sat in the morning shade of a plum tree making a pastel drawing of part of the garden. He had bowed his respects.

'Do I find you well, Lady Frances?' he'd begun, and she'd replied that she was very well indeed and better for seeing him, and bade him sit on the low wall nearby, her heart going pit-a-pat because he'd obviously sought her out.

She'd not been alone in his presence before, although yards away a dozen servants could be seen going about their duties. She'd been surprised at the ease of conversation as he remarked on the pretty skill of her drawing. He'd touched on the beauty of his gardens at Chippenham. 'Which would benefit from your drawing of them, for I am no artist in that respect,' he'd said with a self-deprecating chuckle. She'd playfully scoffed at his admission and it was as though they'd known each other all their lives.

'What do you think of John Russell?' she now asked Mary as they came in from the dusk.

Mary had got over her huff and was now eager to talk. 'I think he is a most agreeable person. The Russells are one of the wealthiest families in England.'

'What has that to do with his agreeableness?' laughed Frances.

Mary looked flustered. 'I merely thought . . .' She hesitated briefly before plunging in. 'I thought that he would make an admirable husband for someone, some day.'

'Someone?' challenged Frances. 'Who would you have in mind?'

'I've no idea!' Mary shot at her, and hurried on ahead of her.

Catching up with her, Frances took her arm. 'Are you matchmaking again, Mall, or have our parents been scheming on my behalf?'

'It has been spoken of,' admitted Mary after some hesitation. She eyed her sister cautiously. 'Mama was saying you ought not stay a widow overlong. She spoke of John Russell being young and unaffianced.'

'She spoke of it in your presence?'

'Tom and I chanced to be with them at the time.'

'And who else?' She was beginning to feel angry. Having her heart race at the thought of John Russell was one thing. Having her life ordered in regard to him was another. 'Who else, Mall?' she prompted. It had all the appearances of a family conspiracy, and she was not even being consulted!

'Dick and Doll,' came the reply.

She drew in an angry breath. 'Half the family present, but not me!'

Mary looked a little abashed. 'There's no plot, Frankie. It was merely during the course of conversation, and you happened not to be present. No one mentioned anything of marriage contracts.' She broke off in remorse. 'Oh, Frankie, I didn't mean to upset you.'

'I'm not upset,' she sighed. 'But I'd prefer to be included in family discussions, as you are. I feel excluded because of my unwed state.'

'It was nothing like that,' protested Mary, moving towards the staircase to the upper floor, where she and Tom had their private rooms and where she might be left in peace.

Frances called to the departing figure. 'Nevertheless, there seems to be great thought in everyone's mind concerning myself and John Russell.'

But some of her annoyance had faded, and in fact it was pleasant to think of Sir John Russell suing for her hand in marriage. It had not yet come to that, of course. He'd mentioned nothing, and any speculation her parents might have they were keeping to themselves for the while.

Even so, for all she was a widow of barely six months and still deeply felt the loss of Robert, she couldn't help experiencing a twinge of excitement. Not that she was head over heels in love with John Russell – handsome though he was – for his very correctness ruled out passion, but she was too young to continue being a widow for long. To be married again struck her as being quite an attractive prospect.

Thurloe made a visit to Lady Cromwell.

His lips beneath the drooping moustache were drawn down. His long sallow features were anxious. 'I think it best we bring His Highness back to Whitehall. He would receive better attention being near Parliament, and I would be constantly near him.'

He watched her nod, her round face full of concern. Thankfully, she had no idea what was really in his mind. He, like many others, was worried by the matter of a successor should his chief die. True, he'd been near to dying many times before, from the fever that plagued him and his recurrent stone, and though Thurloe had no wish to be too hasty in considering the matter of a successor, it would be better were Cromwell in London so that he, Thurloe, wouldn't constantly have to travel out to Hampton Court to see him.

'I trust to your judgement, Mr Thurloe, implicitly,' Elizabeth said now.

During the week, Oliver went by boat down to Whitehall, knowing he would rest better in his old familiar rooms. Elizabeth was left behind for the moment, the summer being fine, and she so happy at Hampton Court, and without her to remind him constantly of Betty, he was sure of a return to health.

Sure enough, the pain from his stone did subside to a degree, though the feverishness continued, despite his doctors being called.

'They think they alone can set my health right,' Cromwell complained to Thurloe. 'They should learn that it is the Lord who will see me safely back to health, despite their intolerable draughts and potions and bleeding cups. I've recovered from worse fevers, and I will with God's help recover again, so tell them to let me rest!'

It seemed he was right. By Thursday, he was up again, taking dinner with men such as Whitelock, discussing business, even dealing with an incensed Fairfax, much to Richard's anger when he heard of it.

'The man should be hanged!' Richard shouted as he burst into his youngest sister's bedchamber, where Frances and Dorothy were sitting chatting. 'He takes advantage of Father's weakened condition by storming in upon him and causing such an unpleasant scene that I wonder why Father didn't have him thrown into the Tower along with his son-in-law!'

'Who are you speaking of?' asked Dorothy.

'Sir Thomas Fairfax,' he threw at her as he dropped into one of the small, silk-upholstered elbow chairs. 'Now Father is at Whitehall, it's taken for granted he can give audience to whoever feels the need. He generously granted Fairfax an interview, and this is how he abuses it, by shouting and stamping. I was witness to his antics and was disgusted by it.'

'What was the cause?' asked Frances. She saw him take a deep breath to compose himself, his head thrown back, one leg doubled beneath the chair, the other sticking straight out in front.

'Fairfax came pleading Villiers' release from the Tower. I can sympathise with his anger. The man has been there ever since his capture after making off with Mary Fairfax. I cannot see what crime there was in marrying the girl – the whole thing is a petty display of wills.'

'Papa is Lord Protector,' reminded Frances, laying aside the small piece of cross-stitch she was working on. 'To go against the wishes of a Head of State can be counted as treason.'

'That I would contest, had I a mind to,' said Dick, coming to an upright position in his chair. 'A king perhaps – not a protector. But my argument is with Fairfax storming in, flying into a passion, throwing his cloak over his arm and cocking his hat at him as a man might do to an equal in the centre of Leadenhall Street! Done in the sight of everyone present in the audience chamber. His conduct was as if my father had been a mere servant.'

'That was imprudent,' sighed Doll. 'I too am surprised your father didn't have him arrested.'

'I think he's too exhausted from these attacks of ague. The old spark has gone out of him. Extinguished, and I don't think it will come back. To take such insult and do nothing – that's not like Father, for all he has been lenient in the past. But his leniency always had a motive.'

'True,' murmured Frances with previous knowledge of how patient her father could be before delivering his *coup de grâce*.

'This is something far more worrying,' he went on.

126

'It is as if in some way he feels the breath of death about him.'

'Dick!' Censure came on both women's lips, while Frances added fearfully, 'Don't say such things!'

Sadly he shook his head. 'I don't like the look of him, Frankie. Fairfax left him drooping in his chair, telling us to let the incident pass. He has dismissed us all and gone to his rooms. He is today lying on his bed saying he must rest. Frankie . . .' Richard leaned forward in his chair. 'Frankie, attend me without crying out. I have the worst feeling that his time is running out. He is about the strangest of quests, commanding Thurloe to send for a certain sealed paper, and I feel it may contain his successor. Who, none knows. Fleetwood had hinted a hope of his own name being mentioned. But as Lord Protector, Father has the right to name his eldest son, though I am not of a mind to want that. If it be Henry, then our father has made the wiser choice.'

Frances found her voice. 'Papa has survived these illnesses before.' But Richard ignored it. He looked at her.

'He has also been dwelling on your future, Frankie. He mentioned but a few days ago that he would not wish to leave this world without knowing you were settled in marriage. He expressed a hope that you might see Henry's brother-in-law, John Russell, in a favourable light. But he is loath at this time to trouble you with marriage contracts. It's these things that worry me about the path his thoughts are taking.'

Frances sat there trying to take in all her brother had said. She tried to think of John Russell but all she could think about was Papa.

'He won't die,' she said shakily. 'He cannot die.'

127

Ten

The storm that had threatened for days finally broke on Monday night on the last but one day of August, with a force such as hadn't been seen by even the oldest person in the country.

After the Fairfax incident, Oliver's recurrent ague had once again struck him, but this time his doctors pessimistically shook their heads against his surviving this one, by far the most violent of his attacks yet.

Elizabeth and her daughters arrived in haste from Hampton Court, and she sat with him through the three days he lay barely conscious and torn by alternate hot and cold sweats that towards Monday began to develop such clogged breathing until he seemed to be on the verge of suffocating.

'The situation is most serious, madam,' Thurloe confided in her. 'I think you should be warned: the doctors fear for his life.'

'He has recovered before from such distempers,' she told him, gazing imploringly into his face. 'Is it so bad this time?'

'I am loath to tell you it is, madam. We must pray most earnestly for God's grace upon him.'

Hers was a quiet woe, yet still hopeful. 'Then we must set tomorrow aside for a day of prayer, Mr Thurloe. I shall beseech the nation to pray for God to be with him in this.'

She told the same to her daughters gathered outside his room, but Frances could feel no faith in that. Hadn't she prayed as earnestly for God to be with Robert and hadn't He forsaken her for all her prayers?

'Mama is too taken up with the power of collective prayer,' she said to her sisters after her mother had gone to see to the arrangements. 'What good did it do for my poor Robert?'

Bridget, with her dour piety undiminished over the years, was quick to reprimand. 'Has your love of the Lord not taught you anything? That He heeds the cries of all His children and turns not His back on any who seek him honestly?'

'I've prayed with all my heart these past days,' retorted Frances, 'but Papa worsens with every hour.'

'Then pray harder!' Bridget's heart-shaped face with its pointy chin grew prim and tight, her neck arched and her back became stiff and straight with her conviction. 'And lose not your faith in Him who brings succour to those who cry earnestly to Him in their need.'

With this she sought her husband's hand and had him press hers reassuringly. 'Do as my wife says,' advised Fleetwood, 'and we will have great assurances of his recovery.'

But as continuous lightning across the country struck down sturdy oaks that had stood for hundreds of years and thunder rolled without pause, as village lanes became torrents of mud, the streets turned into lakes and the wind uprooted trees, tearing tiles and thatch to pieces and demolishing hundreds of chimneys, some swore they felt Cromwell's soul pass over their heads.

As Tuesday dawned with the world swept clean, Oliver opened his eyes to ask feebly if Ludlow had yet come to London to stir up the Army.

'Our prayers are answered!' cried Elizabeth, bidding her family gather about the bed to witness the miracle, and going on her knees, with them all following suit, to give thanks for his having been spared.

'God has shown Himself in a great storm to answer all our prayers,' she said with all reverence.

At his Dublin home, Henry read John Thurloe's letter telling of his continued fears for Cromwell's hope of survival and that Fauconberg might support Henry's claim of succession over his weaker brother Richard. All through his father's illness Thurloe had kept in touch on the subject, but Henry had his own thoughts on it.

'I am aware of his good sense in this,' he said to Elizabeth as he toyed with Thurloe's letter. 'I know I'm considered more capable than Dick, but what he doesn't acknowledge – and I've told him this a thousand times – is that I am weary of office, of constant debt and of this continual game of politics. I'd rather be left to retire to private life, but he constantly dissuades me. Would you dissuade me, my dearest?'

'No, I would not,' she returned emphatically, her slim fingers fondling the fair hair of Oliver, their two-year-old, sitting on her lap. Next to her in his cradle gurgled little Henry, born in March. At her feet four-year-old Elizabeth was playing contentedly. They made such a happy tableau of domesticity that Henry's eyes softened at the sight. Impulsively he came and dropped a kiss on his wife's high forehead then knelt beside her to gaze into her face.

'You would not have me take up my father's baton?'

'My dear heart.' She took her gaze off her children to look at him. 'I'd have you of easy mind without the cares of office your father has strained so hard to achieve. Let us just be happy – that is all I pray for.'

Gently, Henry took her to him, reaching around his brood to do so, Thurloe's letter lying forgotten on the floor.

Two days since the great storm, and Oliver's improvement had been brief indeed. They gathered around his bed as if around a dying king, the political, materialistic Council of State. Who would be his successor?

Frances eyed them balefully as she sat to one side with the rest of the family; those who loved him, knew him best and who forgave all his faults, awaited the moment to be left alone with the beloved head of the family.

Like them, she prayed for him. She prayed that he be granted his life, be his old self again. Although she knew her prayers were in vain, he seemed still so in command of himself – a man worn down by fever, a shadow of his former self, old at sixty, yet even now his presence was a force that could not be ignored. His voice when he spoke still had strength, though mostly he spoke to himself, and mostly concerning his grace with God, his love of God, his faith in God's love for him as His servant. In this, those about him were aware that he knew his end wasn't far off.

'My work is done,' Frances heard him say, causing tears to flow from her. Amazing how strong that voice sounded as he continued in monotone as though in prayer.

'My work is done, but God will be with His people. Thou hast made me, though unworthy, an instrument to do them some good and Thee service, and many of them have set too high a value upon me, though others wish and would be glad of my death. Ah, Lord, however Thou do dispose of me, continue to do good for them. Children, live like Christians. I leave you the covenant to feed upon.'

Hearing his words, Mary burst into a flood of weeping and had to be taken to a corner to regain control of her emotions while her mother leaned over him.

'Dearest husband,' she could be heard whispering. 'There is no need to worry yourself. See, you have gained in strength.'

She lifted his hand then released it, but instead of dropping to the coverlet it remained steadily upheld. For a while he gazed at it.

'This,' he said slowly, 'has been guided by God all these years. Faith in the covenant is my only support. Yet if I believe not, He remains faithful. Ah, we sin, and if we sin we have an Advocate with the Father, Jesus Christ the Righteous. Ah, Elizabeth, I think I am the poorest wretch that lives . . .'

'No, my dear. Never.'

'But I love God,' he continued. 'Or rather I am beloved of God. Herein is love. Not that we love God but that He loved us and sent us propitiation for our sins . . . We love Him because He first loved us . . .'

The words faltered. The hand fell upon the quilt and lay there like a weak, white fish. But as Elizabeth took it, his grip on her fingers became firm. 'God is good, my dear. Never forget. God is good.'

The voice faded. Thurloe and one of Cromwell's

doctors came forward to look, then Thurloe stepped back.

'His strength of will is remarkable,' he said. His comment seemed to bear this out, as Cromwell appeared to rally enough to talk on religion to those gathered about his bed. But after a while it was obvious his words were faltering, his voice growing hoarse. He began to toss so restlessly that Elizabeth got up to pour some water for him from a little jug by the bed, the dignitaries respectfully moving aside for her. The room was hushed as she bent over her husband. 'Oliver, my dear,' she urged. 'Drink a little. Then you might sleep easier.'

He looked up at her and there was a smile on his lips. 'It is not my design,' he said clearly, 'to drink or to sleep, but to make what haste I can to be gone.'

Doctor Blake took her to one side. 'He has made his will, ma'am. In that he is content.'

'He is as close as that,' she returned. Her strength was marvellous to watch, as she took her husband's hand firmly in hers, smiling down at him, and there she remained with her hand holding his.

It was Friday morning, the third day of September. Dawn came in clear, fresher than before the recent storm. In the darkened room the onlookers – family and ministers alike – sat on, waiting. Still Cromwell clung to what was left of his life, but it was obvious to all that he was about to join his Maker.

Frances heard someone ask if he would name Richard as his successor, and heard him murmur, 'Yes.' Just the single word: 'Yes.' In consternation for her brother she shot a glance at him. He was standing upright and tense. His face had gone pale, and her heart went out to him. Poor Dick, he looked as unprepared to follow his father's great office as anyone could be.

She wanted to cry out, No, leave him alone, he hasn't the strength. But her father's voice came strong and clear, as if Mama holding his hand again had put strength into him.

'I tell you I shall not die this hour. I'm sure of it. I speak the words of truth upon surer ground than Galen or your Hippocrates furnish you with.'

Frances took him to be speaking to his doctors, almost admonishing them.

An hour later, almost as if he had predicted that an hour would pass, there was sudden activity around the bed, and along with the rest, she was ushered forward, the men of the Council of State moving back for his loved ones to gather. It was then Frances knew that her father's great strength would no more light his beloved nation's path.

For half an hour they sat around him watching him fade slowly, and just before he slid into final unconsciousness, he murmured weakly, 'Go on cheerfully. My own faith is all in God.'

They watched as he slept for another hour without stirring, and even the doctors were unsure of the time when sleep became death, so quietly did her father, her most beloved father, slip away from them all and from his cares of office. His watch over his country was at an end.

Eleven

'Why did *I* have to be our father's successor?' Richard's fine, narrow face held a strained look as he prowled his youngest sister's sitting room at Whitehall while she and Dorothy watched.

'Already they gather with their cursed insults.' He stopped abruptly to glare at them. 'I chanced upon a group of ill-tongued rogues sniggering together – and Father's funeral hardly done! – to overhear one remark that some fellow, whoever he was, was as queer as Dick's hatband! It's not the first time I heard that remark. I confronted the rascal but he turned bright crimson and mumbled that I'd misheard him.'

'What did he mean?' asked Dorothy innocently.

'It means I'm subjected to crude and unsubstantial jests.'

'Papa was subjected to much the same,' Frances reminded him, 'throughout his political life, as is any statesman. But he was always able to cast it off. "A feather in the hat!" he would say.'

With a deep sense of love and longing to have him back with them, she'd quoted her father's favourite phrase for anything trivial. But longing was overlaid with annoyance at her brother in showing that spine-lessness which the people – and not just his enemies –

were beginning to say of him.

He'd inherited an exacting office, one his father had taken upon himself and had never shirked, even to his grave. She'd expected Dick to settle to it in time. It was never easy to follow in another's footsteps, to uphold that previously achieved. She had been ready to forgive Dick his nervous hesitation, his first fumbling errors. But his failure to take even those first steps had brought deep disappointment not only to her but to the whole country. Few displayed any confidence in him.

She shrugged wearily as he continued to bemoan his lot. Perhaps he needed a little longer to show his mettle – he'd only been in office for two months so far. After all, it had taken a long while before their father's own greatness had come upon him – so long a while that people forgot his obscure beginnings.

She was too tired to bother herself just now with what might be premature assumptions. She was drained from the drawn-out ritual from which they had only just returned: a parody of a funeral for the benefit of the nation.

The body of her father had been taken for burial long ago. This funeral today had held a wax effigy of him, the cortège taking a seven-hour tortuous route through London's streets in the bone-chilling cold of a late November afternoon so that all men could view the open hearse with its wax likeness of their great Lord Protector. But the Abbey had not been provided with enough candles or heating, despite huge amounts of money spent on the rest of the sumptuous arrangements.

No greater funeral had been seen since that of James I, and despite the cold, crowds had turned out in their thousands, the soldiers' red coats covered black, the flags furled and enclosed in dark Cyprus foliage, a symbol of mourning. Two by two, the poor of Westminster had headed the procession, followed by the servants of high-ranking families, then her father's own servants, everyone in special mourning gowns. Then followed the great men, also in mourning, and finally the hearse with its wax image.

That absurd ritual had much to do with the poor preservation of the body proper. For all the aromatic embalming potions, evil fluids of the body had broken through so that a hurried private burial had been necessary within a fortnight of her father's death.

Frances was appalled by the hypocrisy that had followed – the lying-in-state at Somerset House, not even a body for the public to view, but one of wax, with eyes made of glass, Papa's sparse beard and moustache made of animal hair, the figure lain upon a splendid catafalque shrouded by black velvet and lit by a glittering abundance of candles.

Four rooms, their walls draped in black velvet with gold fringes and tassels, had been set aside for the people to pass through in order to view the re-creation of a custom once reserved only for royal persons. Even the railings to keep back the spectators had been draped in black.

The figure was clad in a suit of black velvet, a coat trimmed with ermine and a robe of purple and gold lace, a jewelled belt and engraved sword, a sceptre in the left hand, on the waxen head an ermine-trimmed cap of purple velvet and behind the head a golden chair bearing an imperial crown. Frances had to hold back tears of mortification at the sight of the crown more than all the rest.

At each side had been placed her father's four standards as Lord Protector and at each corner there had been huge carvings of lions and dragons, all lit by eight candles in silver holders reaching a height of eight feet. The business was made more ludicrous, and, for her, blasphemous, by the figure being repositioned according to royal custom in an upright posture, the glass eyes open and on his head the imperial crown as a sign of the soul having passed through Purgatory and entered Heaven.

The whole thing had been distasteful. What was especially obscene was that, on his death, a king had been made of a man who had steadfastly refused to be king.

'Had Richard's father become king,' Dorothy said later to Frances, 'this adversity over his succession would not have arisen. He'd be king by right and his life would be so much simpler. As it is, he is in a turmoil as Head of State without the rights of kingship.'

Richard looked woebegone. 'Had he prepared me better,' he groaned as he dropped down into a chair, 'I'd not be at such a loss now.'

Frances turned on him. 'That's unfair, Dick! Papa gave you every opportunity to enter politics and take responsibilities.' Words came tumbling from her in a torrent. 'You were made Lord of Trade and Navigation in 1655 and the following year you were returned as Member for Hampshire as well as the University of Cambridge, and last year you were elected Papa's successor for the Chancellorship of Oxford. You had ample chances, had you but stirred yourself more with affairs of state rather than playing gentleman farmer . . .'

140

'No, Frankie!' cried Dorothy in alarm. 'You mustn't blame him.'

'I do blame him,' said Frances. 'Had he shown any gift, Papa would have given him Ireland to govern instead of Henry. He would have been confident of the Protectorship.'

'Henry doesn't do so well – he's up to his ears in debt,' pouted Dorothy.

'That wasn't his doing,' Richard chimed in, prudently stopping short of saying anything that would have spoken against his dead father. But Frances was well aware of how short of cash Papa had kept his Viceroy in Ireland, and was glad their mother wasn't present to hear Richard at this moment.

Mama had gone to her rooms to take a little opium to soothe away a headache brought on by the chill of this exacting day, hoping for sleep to smother the pangs of her loss, which had been renewed by the mockery of the state funeral. Her loss surrounded her like a shroud, though she had refused to weep in public. The rest of them had wept, though, even Bridget. Mary had been so overcome these past two months that her husband, hardly knowing what to do with her, had at one time threatened to go eighty miles out of town! But the closest Frances had seen her mother come anywhere near to tears was a week before the official state funeral, when she'd spoken of her forty years of marriage.

'In perfect contentment and harmony,' she'd sighed, conveniently overlooking those long, lonely hours of his preoccupation with Parliamentary affairs and the times she'd complained of not being consulted on the simplest things, and her intense jealousy when beautiful vivacious women had commanded his attentions and received them willingly from him.

'Without my dearest captain at this helm,' she'd sighed, 'I am a ship without anchor or rudder. At the mercy of the tides I must endeavour to regain my course as best I can – for your brother's sake, until he can take his place at that now unmanned helm . . . if he can.'

Those last words had reflected her understanding of Dick, himself a ship at sea, dreaming only of the wealth his role could bring yet dreading the role itself.

With tiresome regularity she would say, 'We must put our trust in God, who directs us all,' or, 'It pleased the Lord to take your father to his rest – now I pray He be at *your* side, to guide you in all things and make you His humble servant to do His work among your people, as did your father.'

Dick had sighed and placated her with promises that he would. Then he'd hurried off out of reach of her tongue to those splendid apartments he'd been given at Whitehall, which had been lavishly fitted to suit the fine taste of His Serene Highness Lord Richard, Lord Protector. That, though, was about as far as his role had gone to date.

'And what now of your plans, Frances, without husband or father?' The question took her by surprise. It was December, and John Russell had come to call upon her, as he had quite often since the loss of her father. In her Whitehall apartments he now sat opposite her, as always very correct, making no overtures towards her. For the best part of an hour they'd chatted about this and that, his manner one of brotherly affection and his conversation lively but fraternal.

In a surge of hope she thoughtlessly blurted out the silliest response to the question he'd asked. 'I've not given much thought to it.'

Immediately she'd said it she wanted to bite off her tongue. She'd done little else *but* give it thought. Over the months her hopes of his asking just such a question of her had grown, hopes dulled awhile by the loss of her father, but again returning to occupy her every waking moment. And all she could say now was something utterly ridiculous.

She had mentioned her hopes to Dorothy, expecting they would get back to Richard. It was correct that he negotiate for her as head of the family now, but there'd been no response as far as she could see, his mind more likely being preoccupied with affairs of state rather than with Frances' future. Thus John Russell's question coming out of the blue brought a sudden flood of expectation. And all she could reply was that she'd not given much thought to it! Dear God!

He had been studying her for what seemed an age, with a faint smile playing about his firm, wide mouth.

'Then may I suggest,' he said in a quiet, almost fatherly tone, 'that you give some thought to it? I am mindful of the unhappy state of your family at this time. Your brother, much as he is a most agreeable man, has not the attributes your father had. Forgive me, Frances – it must be said. There is a danger your brother may bring this country into confusion by his inability to rule with the strength your father possessed. There are those who seek vengeance for your father's past deeds and would see your family ruined. In this I would have you think of your own future, my dear. It could be of the utmost importance to you. And to me.'

143

'To you?'

'Frances, I am mindful of your unhappy state – so recently, and in quick succession, you have lost a dear husband, a dear sister and a dear father. With all my heart I would remedy that unhappiness were you to allow me to.'

'Your pardon?' she asked, uncertain how to reply.

'Surely you must know what is in my heart?'

'I cannot tell what is in your heart,' she evaded, fearing to interpret wrongly lest she be disappointed.

'That it is filled with the greatest respect and love for you. Further, I've asked your brother for your hand in marriage, Frances, if you will accept.'

She was on the verge of laughing and crying both at the same time. Had he but known, there'd been no need for such formality, for such a roundabout proposal of marriage – all he had to have said was that he wanted her for his wife, and she'd have needed no other coaxing.

Her reaction was having an adverse effect on him. He was frowning as though hearing a rejection, and she hastily sought to right the error, but, so as not to appear too frivolous, she made her reply formal. 'I do readily accept and thank you, John, for the pleasure it gives me.'

For a fleeting second she had a recollection of the reply she'd given to Robert when he'd proposed marriage: 'Oh, yes, my darling, yes – yes!' And he'd swept her into his arms as they'd sunk to the ground with passionate kisses . . .

The sad longing passed over her and was gone, like a fleeting fragrance. How different this was – a formal contract if ever there was one. Yet she wanted to be

John's wife, even if her regard for him was nothing like the burning desire that she'd had for Robert.

Perhaps there were many kinds of love, and this agreement to be John Russell's wife was just one – a more mature sort, perhaps. If so, she must put aside dreams of romance. That was all in the past – she had outgrown them and must face this new growth towards maturity.

He did not sweep her into his arms. He simply rose from his chair and came to take her hands firmly between his. They felt exceptionally warm.

'You have made me very happy, Frances,' he said solemnly.

There came a mad desire to leap up, to reach out at him and draw him to her, force him to take her in his arms and press his lips to hers. A voice in her head cried out, 'Hold me! I've promised to be your wife. Love me then!'

But she only smiled, lowering her head as though she was blushing.

They were married at Richard's home in Hursley. It had been John's suggestion – he had always had a fondness for the place, and Frances quite agreed with him. Set amid the rolling Hampshire downs, with its lovely beech woods, it possessed a certain tranquillity, and she understood her brother's reluctance to forsake it and take up residence at Whitehall.

To her relief and joy, she was discovering that she and John were proving compatible in all things, though it was strange being addressed as Lady Russell.

From the first, John took charge of everything. Where she had been the one to make decisions with Robert, she now found her new husband making them for her. It was rather a nice feeling, and, as he was most considerate of her in all things, she found it suited her well enough.

The only drawback was that he wasn't a passionate man. More than once she would hark back in her mind to past loves – the first in secret, the clandestine meetings, the joyous agitation of guilt, love taken by a selfish man and by its very sinfulness destined not to endure; the second a true sense of sharing, sweet and gentle and blessed, and which should have lasted her the rest of her life had not cruel death ended it. And now this, a union borne more out of respect for a fine man than any deep passion for him.

With the hope that in time it might grow to be a more passionate thing, she knew that even if it didn't, it would at least endure, like one of those sturdy, ancient beeches she could see from her brother's house.

They went to Chippenham, the Russell family home, for Christmas. The vast family – John the eldest of fourteen children, very few of whom had died, and those married swelling the numbers even more – made her most welcome. Their immense warmth towards her more than compensated for the cold, featureless Cambridgeshire countryside, its grey winter sky as flat as the ploughed, black, empty fields.

But the house too, a fine manor, had a welcoming aspect, her new husband's pleasant and easy company merely adding to its idyllic charm. Although their marriage still lacked the wonderful pleasure she'd known with Robert, by the time they returned to London in February, she knew she was with child. This ultimate sense of being a woman fulfilled had been the one thing she'd so far lacked, and she knew a deep gratitude and love towards John, more than passion could ever have instilled.

Returning to London was a shock. While she had been cocooned in Chippenham these several weeks, England had grown increasingly dissatisfied with its new Protector. Now she found herself once again exposed to the hard light of politics and dissention.

'I'm at my wits' end,' Richard told them, hardly had they set foot in Whitehall. It was a very different place from the one they had left. Her mother had unexpectedly moved herself and her servants to St James's Palace across the park. John Claypole, concerned for a woman alone, had accompanied her. Bridget and her family were back at Stoke Newington, and Mary was at her London home at Fauconberg House.

Never had the family apartments felt so deserted. In this great empty palace of Whitehall, Richard ruled in splendid isolation, finding it far from pleasant, judging by his bleating as he greeted Frances and her husband.

'There's disaffection everywhere. I'm so low in funds as to have practically nothing to call upon, and indeed owe to the Treasury.'

'How could you get yourself into such a muddle?' Frances scolded, reaping an instant petty show of peevishness.

'If you knew how deep in debt Father had been, you wouldn't accuse me of mishandling accounts. He spent and spent on lavish spectacle, and this is how he has left me.'

'How can you say that?' she fumed back at him. 'Did any see Papa dressed in gaudy fashion or laying out on things for himself?'

'He had no care for clothes, that's true,' railed Dick,

'yet he spent vast amounts of Treasury money on show and pomp. He hardly ceased to spend on such things here at home, yet left Henry in poverty in Ireland.'

'That's not true! He sent funds regularly to Henry.'

'But never enough to meet his needs as Lord Deputy. You have but to ask Charles Fleetwood. He has letters from Henry saying how much Ireland kept him poor, and complaining against Father's stinginess. And now I have not only my own debts, I have those he has left me. That's my father's true legacy to me! Now the country is calling me to account, and they call me Tumbledown Dick. I'm in such a plight that I dare not even renew Henry's commission except on the terms my Council acquiesces. They dictate to me at every turn, yet blame me for all that is wrong.'

He looked so helpless that she forgot to be cross with him. 'Then show them you are as strong as Papa was,' she said severely.

'How?'

'By coming to your own decisions and keeping to them. Then you will regain the nation's respect, as Papa once did.'

His handsome face remained pathetically downcast. 'The battle is lost hardly has it begun, Frankie. I can't don Father's shoes. All I wish is to be left in peace, to follow the life I've always loved – a country gentleman with my horses and my dogs and my hawks.'

While still glorying in the Protectorship, thought Frances ruefully. All he had to do was resign, hand over to his more capable brother, Henry, and his woes would be at an end. But she said nothing of this aloud as he continued.

'I've not the genius for government, nor have I

friends or even treasure to support me. The new Parliament is against me, clamouring for Father's debts to be paid, which money I do not have, and I must throw in my lot with the Army Council for protection. But I can scarce trust even them.'

'Why has Mama left Whitehall for St James's Palace?' she demanded, cutting across his laments.

'She feels safer,' came the distracted reply.

'Safer?'

'I wrote to you of it the day she left. Have you not read it?'

She made no reply. But later, in the carriage on the way to her mother's new home at St James's Palace, she turned angrily to her husband. 'Did you know of this? Of all that was going on here?'

At his brief affirmative nod, anger exploded.

'Why couldn't you tell me? To open my letters and not tell me . . .'

'It was to protect you, my dear.'

'I need no such protection, John,' she burst in. 'Why do you treat me like a child? I'm not a weakling to be shielded from the world. I am the daughter of the Lord Oliver Cromwell who led this country ably and with pride in the face of all adversity and the worst his enemies could do. How dare you feel the need to protect me from the worst his enemies can now do?'

'You were so happy, I wanted not to spoil it.'

She'd never seen him crestfallen before, had never thought herself capable of speaking her mind to him with such force. With a stab of remorse she moderated her tone. 'But to find things in such turmoil . . . Oh, my dear, how could you keep me in sublime ignorance? And to open my letters . . .'

'That was wrong of me.'

In a surge of desperation she turned to him, anger interrupted by a new and stronger fear of the future. 'Richard is so weak. How can he prevail if the country is turning against him?'

In the lurching coach she felt for his hand; at the first touch, he took hers and brought it to his lips. 'I have a sturdy, courageous wife,' he murmured solemnly, 'on whom I can depend in all things. I was long a champion of your father's case for all I began a Royalist. But your brother, my dear, is different, and is not of the stuff to carry the burden placed on him by the death of your gracious father. Should he fall, we mustn't be brought down with him. I think your sister, Lady Fauconberg, is of the same thought. I can foresee a great flood of change, and we must flow with it until we reach tranquil shores. The Old Cause is gone forever, Frances.'

She brought her free hand up to touch his firm, narrow cheek, and a surge of love for him rippled through her, taking her by surprise.

'I shouldn't have railed at you as I did,' she said softly. 'I know you had my well-being at heart, and I will be guided by you in all things lest we fight each other instead of our enemies.'

She wanted to say, because I love you. But not yet – it would come.

John's prediction of a new turn of opinion seemed not far wrong. The senior Lady Cromwell was hardly able to keep the tears from her ageing eyes as she received him and Frances.

'I shall not remain here,' she said as they sat in

a sumptuous room. 'Parliament has queried by what authority I have been granted twenty thousand pounds a year for my lifetime. I had thought to assist Dick with his debts, but now . . .' She heaved a sigh of resignation. 'Now it seems I must deliver it up to Parliament.'

'How do they expect you to live?' cried Frances, her mind already on the vast Russell fortunes. As long as she was John's wife, her mother would want for nothing.

She told her so, out of his hearing, but her mother shook her head. 'I have a little fortune of my own. Jewels and pictures and a quantity of gold that I managed to bring with me. They are hidden safe in the warehouse of a fruiterer in Thames Street. In time I shall export them out of the country and will exist very well off it.' Leaning forward, she patted her daughter's hand. 'I do thank you for the kind concern you have for me, but you see I have no need of it.'

Not long afterwards, her mother was dispossessed of St James's and went to live at the Cockpit, her old home before the family had so grandly transferred to Whitehall Palace during her husband's Lord Lieutenantship.

'If the truth be known,' Frances confided in Mary, during one of their frequent calls on each other, heartily renewed now that they were both in London, 'Mama is happier at the Cockpit than ever she was in that great rambling palace. Do you recall how she had those great apartment rooms divided into smaller, humbler ones and how we all complained so? She has ever been a plain person of propriety.'

Mary gave a firm sigh. 'At least the Army has

151

made a good settlement upon her, and she'll want for nothing.'

God grant it be so, prayed Frances, and was sure He would for such a quiet and gentle soul.

Twelve

It was a new experience, this life growing inside her. Unbelievable how well she felt, hardly any discomfort, and what little there was she bore with joy. As for the sickness that women were expected to suffer on waking in the morning, it was scarcely enough to bother her.

'Henry's wife suffered terribly from it when carrying little Henry,' Frances said, nibbling sweetmeats with Mary in the sunny parlour at Fauconberg House. Her sister-in-law's second son, born at Dublin Castle, was now just over a year old. 'Poor Elizabeth says she was martyr to sickness.'

'Dorothy too,' said Mary, seeking her favourite sweet from the little glass dish. 'Although I must say, none of her children are particularly robust. It's perhaps all that sickness that does it.'

Frances nodded sadly. 'Poor Doll, she has such misfortune.'

The child Dorothy had named for herself had died in December, but there had been so much tragedy of late that the loss of the little one had gone almost unnoticed except by the mother. But Doll had again been with child at the time; Anna, born six weeks ago in March, had been some consolation to her.

'At least,' observed Frances, 'she's proving a strong child.'

'To my mind,' said Mary, sucking vigorously on her sweet, 'she does have her children too much one after the other.'

Frances turned her gaze idly to the garden beyond the tall window, brilliant in the May sunshine. Although she spent much of her time at Chippenham, where the countryside was bright with young spring growth and full of pleasant interest, she had need to be in London to be near Mary and Mama as well as Dick and his family – especially Dick, who was a terrible worry to her.

'What of our brother in Whitehall?' she asked, prudently moving from the subject of babies as she noticed a bleak expression steal over Mary's face. Tom and Mary still had no children, though they'd been married these eighteen months. It was best not to rub salt into the wound, with Mary inclined to become a little tight-faced should the subject of children be brought up at the wrong time. Mary was tight-faced now, but this time it was because of her sister's last question.

'He sits in his palace like one of its cornerstones – unmoved by government or public opinion. Mama is in fear of his arrest, but he manages to set Army against Parliament without stirring a limb.'

'John fears it could bring another civil war.'

'I doubt that,' said Mary. 'Dick has let it be known he will not have a drop of blood spilt to preserve his greatness, which he says is itself a burden to him.'

'What he says and what the nation does are two separate things,' said Frances a little archly, recalling how different it had been when her father had been Lord Protector. 'As for greatness . . .' She let the rest go unsaid.

154

From the day the Republicans had formed their Parliament it had been a tug of war between him and them, with the Army – to whom he'd run for protection – intervening occasionally, though he dared not trust even them.

'He *is* Papa's successor,' she added. 'For all he's a mere shadow of him, he was chosen. Everyone agreed to it. And now this. What will he do? What *can* he do? Papa would have fought them tooth and nail.' Vehemently she threw her half-eaten sweetmeat out through the open window.

'I think he'll remain at Whitehall,' said Mary a little scathingly. 'Charles Fleetwood has advised him that if he does he will be taken good care of under the Army's protection. He has told him that the Republicans cannot harm him or arrest him while his Army is behind him.'

Frances had calmed down enough to select a piece of licorice, to which she was very partial. 'I don't trust Fleetwood. We all know he hoped to succeed to the Protectorship.'

'Be that as it may,' said Mary, 'Parliament is promising to pay all our brother's debts the moment he vacates Whitehall.'

'It would mean relinquishing the Protectorship. He cannot do that.'

'Exactly.'

'Then he must stay on.'

'But in penury. He is broke. He lives there in splendid poverty.'

'We must help him.' Frances got out of her chair to walk about the room. 'We're both wealthy. Surely we could find enough funds between us to tide him over this.'

155

From the comfort of her silk-upholstered chair, Mary watched her pace. 'Be sensible, Frankie. The wealth belongs to our husbands' families. In no manner can we demand even a small portion of it.'

When Richard finally made his appearance, having made sufficient effort to get out of his chair in the spacious if half-furnished salon he and Dorothy occupied, he told Parliament the same as he had before, almost word for word: 'I'm ready to comply the moment Parliament honours its promise to pay all debts incurred during my office and those of my father, which have nothing to do with me, for I regret I've no money to pay either of them.'

'What did they say?' Dorothy asked anxiously when he returned to sprawl in his chair again.

'They merely took their leave,' he told her. 'What else could they do? I have the support of the Army and they cannot throw me out.'

'They could arrest you for debt.'

'I've told you,' he sighed as she cuddled little Anna to her as though to defend her against that possible invasion, 'I have the Army's good protection.'

'And if they turn against you?' She shuddered. 'They could, Dick. And you are well aware how quickly they can change sides. Your father was ever holding them at bay.'

'They've no love for Republicans. They are my father's men and they remember his Model Army and how he made them proud.'

'But they are not *your* men, Dick. Not truly.'

The words sent a small shiver of uncertainty through him, and he felt angry with her for being the cause.

156

Falling into a sulk, he refused to speak to her any more on it.

Even so, it seemed he was right in his assumption. He was soon the recipient of another visit, this time from his father's cousin, Lord Chief Justice St John, insisting on a positive answer from him.

'You see?' he told Dorothy in triumph. 'Parliament is growing fearful of some revolution in my favour. Fleetwood was right. The worst they can do is deprive me of the government, but then they must settle a fortune on me, adequate to my modest wishes. And my modest wishes can be as expensive as need be. They have promised it.'

'They keep on promising it!' Dorothy burst out, surprising him with her vehemence. 'But we see nothing done. Meantime our creditors clamour at the door to be paid, not only for what you owe but the debt for your father's pompous funeral, still unpaid. We've even had a writ issued against us, and the palace is virtually besieged by all the bailiffs in Middlesex! Think of that, Richard, if you will! And in the name of the good Lord, think of us, your family, where we will be.'

Turning on her heel, she hurried from the room, leaving him staring after her, his frown thoughtful for once. By the end of May, after yet more negotiating, he at last came to terms with the government that apparently satisfied him.

'Provided I send them a submission promising not to disturb the government,' he told her, 'they'll pay all my debts and provide an honourable subsistence for myself and my family. My removal expenses and living expenses of twenty thousand pounds will be advanced to me, and Parliament is taking me under its protection.'

Dorothy's relief was almost pitiful to see as she gazed towards her children as though they'd been reprieved from the gallows.

'Thank the Lord,' she breathed. 'Perhaps now we may go to live at Hursley in peace. I shall be near my parents and I shall never leave it again.'

Joy was short-lived. Within days the Army grandees, jealous of Richard's position, were petitioning that not only the whole of Richard's debts be paid, but also those of his father contracted since December 1653.

Richard looked sick as he faced his wife.

'They're demanding too much. A hundred thousand pounds a year to be settled upon me and my heirs, and a further ten thousand pounds upon my mother, so that a mark of the high esteem that this nation has of the good services done by my father may remain to posterity. That is what they say. But Parliament will never pay such a high sum.'

'You must tell them no!' Dorothy cried in desperation, seeing her beloved home and peace of mind slipping away from her.

But all her pleas went by him. He firmly believed that Parliament would never pay such a high sum. Although the now alarmed Parliament, aware of an Army looking only for an excuse to cause a breach, promised to exempt and secure him from all arrests and debts for the next six months, he held on like a man clinging to driftwood in a tempest.

Even when a few days later an Order came, decreeing that the palace would be cleared of all persons, he refused to move. He sat on, unresponsive, even as the furniture and household goods were taken away. It was the last straw. Dorothy could take no more.

After a heated row with him, during which he behaved more like a recalcitrant child than a man who should be comforting his distraught wife as she burst into tears, she made up her mind. On the ninth of June she ordered a coach to be loaded with as many of her belongings as it could hold, then, with her children, their nurse and a servant, set off for Hursley, leaving Richard to settle his affairs with Parliament in his own way.

The next day, hearing of Doll's frantic departure, Frances, Mary and their mother made haste to Whitehall to visit Richard and give what comfort they could. They found him, a destitute creature, in one of the smaller rooms; it was empty but for a chair, a table and a chest. His servants were gone.

'You see how they have left me?' he mumbled. 'The Parliament in whom I am asked to trust? Not even a plate to eat off.'

'You can't stay here any longer,' his mother reasoned with him as she gazed around at the decorated partitions she'd ordered to be erected so that the original vast rooms would become cosy family ones. These were now planned to be torn down for this government's own habitation as soon as her son departed.

He didn't even heed her words. It was as though he'd lost his wits to drift in a world of his own. 'Thank God we have our sturdy John Thurloe to advise me still,' he rambled on. 'He at least remains loyal to me, as he was to my father, and warns me against the conspiracies of Army and Parliament.'

'You should follow after Doll,' said Frances, feeling as much at a loss as any of them with this vacant-eyed man, once so witty and gallant. His cheeks had become so hollow and his eyes so haunted that she feared for his sanity.

'Leave here,' she urged, 'and go to Hursley.'

But he remained sitting, gazing at nothing, and didn't answer her. Instead, he sighed weightily. 'Poor Thurloe. For his fine loyalty to us, the Republicans are voting to replace him with Mr Thomas Scott as Secretary of State, even though that gentleman knows nothing of the duties of that office – originally a mere clerk to a brewer. You see how much they hate me and want to be rid of me and any who are loyal to me? I lay no store by their promises – nor anyone's. Even Doll forsakes me.'

At this show of self-pity, Frances's husband, who'd accompanied the women here, stepped in angrily.

'You are a fool, sir! Your wife does not forsake you. You forsake her. Get you to Hursley and to her side, man!'

To one as forceful as John Russell, Richard finally nodded in feeble compliance, allowing them all to breathe a sigh of relief.

However, it wasn't to Hursley that he went, but to Hampton Court, to sit out the storm from there.

'He did it on Charles Fleetwood's advice,' a thunder-struck Mary told Frances in private. 'Dick is so gullible. Can't he see that Fleetwood doesn't advise him out of any affection for him? His motives are purely selfish – to frighten the Republicans and secure the Army in their place. He's using our brother for his own ends. He still thinks to take the helm if he can, by bringing down the government – and Dick at the same time. My husband warns he'll not win. He says it will only make the nation more inclined to be done with lost causes, and they will call back Charles Stuart as our king, to bring stability again to England.'

Frances was only half interested. She had more to occupy her mind with than politics and Richard's predicament. Henry and his family, no longer able to remain in Ireland, had come home at the end of June – if home it still was, so long had they been away. The money for their journey had been arranged by Charles Fleetwood – another of his ulterior motives, she suspected. But Henry had had to accept it, not having enough to pay his own way.

He came to stay at Chippenham, which was his wife's home, to a tearful welcome from the whole of the huge Russell family. John was as overjoyed to see his sister again as Frances was to see her brother. Being pregnant, she was also delighted to see Henry's new son, born at Dublin Castle in March, two weeks before Dick and Doll's little Anna at Whitehall.

'He's so strong and healthy,' she cried as three-month-old Henry wriggled in her arms and bawled lustily, stretching his fat little neck so as not to lose sight of his mother, wanting only her arms.

But there had been bad news too. Their daughter Elizabeth, born at Whitehall five years ago, had been unwell throughout the journey and had arrived so desperately ill that she had been put straight to bed and a doctor sent for. 'It is a flux in her insides for which there seems no cure,' Elizabeth told them. 'It's been so this past year. She seems to be fading away before our eyes, and there is nothing we can do.'

Sure enough the child died on the seventeenth of July, her mother taking her loss with the fortitude of one already girded for it, sorrowing yet unable to begrudge the poor suffering mite peace at last. It was pitiful to see Henry trying to comfort her when his own sorrow was too sharp for him to lessen hers. John, too, was downcast and miserable at his sister's grief; indeed the whole family was in mourning.

Frances felt guilty of her own condition and the joy it was bringing her. 'I can't help it,' she said to John when the funeral was over and they had gone to bed, neither of them able to sleep for thoughts of the sad day. 'All I can think about is our own child. I am so happy, yet so in fear that such could happen to us as has happened today. I pray our child will be strong and healthy – that all our children will be so.'

He cuddled her to him. 'Of course they will. Every one.'

But her fears remained strong, spoiling her joy. 'I couldn't bear to lose a child.'

She recalled her mother once saying that woman is made especially to endure the loss of children. Even so, she repeated plaintively, 'I couldn't bear it,' while John tenderly stroked her hair to comfort her.

With the passing months, and with her stomach swollen to such cumbersome size as to make even the briefest exercise an effort, Frances' mind was more on the coming event than politics and her brother's dilemma.

Throughout the summer, Richard had sat in Hampton Court like some exiled potentate, for the most part lonely, but occasionally entertaining a few of his loyal companions. He'd begun to be more like his old self, with his fine clothes and his fine debts, while Doll remained at Hursley.

Much of his time he spent with his hawks and his

horses, until a fall from a horse in August put an end to it. In his eagerness to outride his retinue – as Mary said uncharitably, 'to show everyone that he still had hold of the country's reins' – his horse had leapt short and thrown him into a ditch. His leg was broken so badly that he was certain to limp for the rest of his life.

'Some say he was drunk,' said Mary.

'That's a wicked lie put about by his enemies,' defended Frances.

But Mary no longer had any sympathy for her foolish brother. 'He asks to be ridiculed. He makes himself look ridiculous, and the Royalists – who are daily growing in numbers – have revived that old quip, Tumbledown Dick, with even more truth than before, in my opinion!'

This Frances couldn't refute. There were songs too, lampooning the erstwhile Protector. She heard one such at Chippenham a few days after Mary's scathing opinion of their brother. She was in her bedroom writing to Mary, the window open, when the sound of a man singing came floating up from the yard below. It was a hoarse but pleasant voice, and, her pen poised, she smiled at the jolly tune. But as the words became clearer to her keen ears, her smile faded.

The singer was obviously unaware of a listener as he worked: '. . . and Dick, being lame, rose holding the pommel, not having the wit to get hold of the rein – but the jade did so snort at the sight of a Cromwell, that Dick and his kindred turned footman again . . .'

So angry was she that she dropped her pen and, waddling to the window as fast as her distended stomach would allow, leaned out and yelled down at the man like some fishwife to cease his damned disrespect of her brother, or she would complain to his master and have him dismissed on the spot.

To his credit the man – a thick-set, bucolic fellow – grew red-faced and ducked his head several times in apology before hurrying on to load his cart, while she pulled her head back from the window, furious with herself for her own undignified lack of self-control. She also had a fear that allowing herself to get so upset and behaving as she had could start her labour pains early, for her time was indeed getting close.

Sure enough, an hour later the first slow sensation of discomfort stole over her as she went cumbersomely downstairs with her finished letter to find a servant. At first she thought it was a backache from sitting at an open window, for a slight breeze had sprung up, and September could be a dangerous month for catching chills. But when the pain melted away to return some fifteen minutes later, and this time much sharper, some inner instinct told her that this was no mere backache from some draught.

A flood of fear sent her tottering into the yard to find John. Then she remembered that he'd left some time ago for nearby Newmarket with his father, Sir Francis, on business to do with the estate. Henry and Elizabeth were away too, having left earlier to visit old friends of hers after so long an absence in Ireland.

Frances found herself taken hold of by several maid-servants who came running out to her cries and was led back into the house and the care of Sarah, John's widowed sister.

'All is well,' she soothed, seeing her charge's terror. 'You've nothing to be frightened of.'

They'd struck up a strong friendship, being about

the same age, and both having suffered widowhood. Yet at this moment of onset of labour she felt she was among strangers. There was a desperate longing to have her mother here, or Mary, or even her strong, capable husband.

'I need John,' she whimpered.

Sarah gave a gentle laugh. 'Now what use would he be? He'd only be in the way, as any man is at these times. Let us get you to your bed. I'll send a servant for my mother to come. She is somewhere about the house.'

Consigned into the hands of John's mother, she felt safe again. Plump from bearing fourteen children, Lady Catherine was sweet and kindly and had made Frances welcome from the start. Sending a messenger to fetch the doctor, she instilled Frances with courage for her coming ordeal, talking calmly on this and that as though it were no more than a matter-of-course business. Frances felt she couldn't be in better hands.

Thirteen

1659–60

In all her life Frances had never known any real physical pain. Toothache as a child, of course, to be soothed with clove and a hot onion placed on the offending place, one or two having had to be pulled with the comfort of a little opium, the pain over in but a moment.

She was therefore unprepared for this sort of pain, for all she'd heard the gasps and shrieks of childbirth before. But they had been the gasps and shrieks of another's pain. These pains were hers, and they tore at her very core, as though the life within loathed her so much as to wish only to rip her apart in its effort to be free of her.

For hour after hour it went on, through the night and the next day, while she twisted and writhed – two lives hating each other's existence. Her womb bearing down with such special agony made her need to push at it to be free, but the more she pushed the more she seemed to trap that life inside her.

'I can't!' she shrieked time and time again. 'I can't endure it! Oh, merciful God, deliver me!'

'You can endure it,' encouraged Lady Catherine as Frances peered beseechingly up at those plump, motherly features.

There was the doctor too, he unmoved by her wretched agony, a lifelong witness of birth pains but never himself touched by them, and therefore lacking the sympathy of the woman with her who had been, many times over. 'Come, enough of this.' His tone was severe, commanding. 'This is a woman's lot, so pray to God for strength rather than cry to Him for release.'

Pray? She hardly had energy enough to cry out, much less pray. Drenched with perspiration, her brow sponged at regular intervals, she gripped the bedposts so tightly she was sure they'd break, sturdy oak though they were. But with strength ebbing, there would soon be no energy left to push this child into the world. An unfair disadvantage did God give woman in that when she most needed her strength, it was all used up in her initial agonies. She would not have the energy now. Her child would suffocate in her womb.

There was sudden activity around her, the doctor roaring at her as though she'd done some wrong: 'Bear down, my lady! Bear down!'

Her mother-in-law was holding her hands against the bedpost, but there was no need – she clung so tightly that her nails must leave their impression in the wood forever more. 'Push, my child, with all your might – the babe is almost here.'

'I cannot . . .'

'In God's Holy Name, my lady, do as I say!'

The doctor's voice was unremitting, unforgiving. More in fear of his wrath than fear of death from this involuntary straining down of her whole self from the top of her head to the pit of her stressed loins, she pushed with all her might, but could not hold it.

168

Her breath gave way in a shriek that was unrecognisable to her.

Again and again prevailed upon to repeat that terrible exercise until she thought her veins would burst, Frances was unable to move the enormous thing inside her; she was beyond all endurance, with her breath always failing in that awful shriek. This was how women died in childbirth! cried the mind.

Moments later, with her breath about to fail yet again, she despairing of ever bringing forth this child alive, there came a slithering as though a little wet rabbit had gushed from her, a gush of warmth so sudden and so easy, it seemed hardly possible that a moment ago there had been no way for it to pass. In that moment of birth, the obstruction that had stretched her almost to the point of splitting her in two was no more. In that instant all pain ceased as if it had never been. It was a miracle. Was this what it was like to bring forth a child, the pain put aside and only relief and fulfilment left in its place?

There had been a leaping forward of the two people with her, and she glimpsed a small bluish body held upside down by its feet, like a skinned hare hung to ripen. It was so momentary that she thought she'd imagined it. There came a sharp smack followed by a thin mewling. That second of fear for her baby's chances of life fell away, replaced by sheer joy as that first thin cry became lustier, demanding.

'A boy!' exclaimed Lady Catherine. 'A handsome, sturdy boy!'

'Let me see. Oh, let me see him.'

'Patience, my dear,' laughed Lady Catherine.

Moments later the child, wrapped tightly in a sheet,

his fine fuzz of hair still wet against his skull, a streak of blood smeared thinly across his fat little cheek, was laid in her eager arms as she fell back, exhausted but happy.

'He is the cleanest born I have ever seen,' cried her mother-in-law admiringly. 'And already robust.'

And he was, twisting his little red face instinctively towards the scent of mother, the squashed lips making sucking sounds already looking for milk. And so very handsome – his father's fine features were already evident.

Love flowed from Frances to her first-born – love and pride. She was a mother. 'We will have lots of sons,' she said sleepily as John tiptoed into the room, his face aglow.

'I fear the labour was hard for you, my sweet.'

But she shook her head, all thought of her pain dimming. 'Not at all,' she told him.

Reassured, he fondled the infant's hand, the tiny fingers already gripping instinctively at his thumb. 'We should call him Oliver, your father's name.'

Frances frowned. 'There are enough Cromwells.'

The hardness in her voice made even Frances wonder for a moment, and she knew he was surprised too. But some knowledge deep inside was telling her that her family's day was over, that the very name would never again sit well on the lips of this nation. She gave an involuntary shudder – so much for all that which her father had achieved.

But the next minute she was smiling. 'Our son is a Russell. See how like you he is already? There is no Cromwell in him at all. We must give him an entirely new name. Your second brother, who died when you were a boy – his name was never given to any other of your brothers, as is normally done. We shall name him William, in honour of your brother.'

John smiled indulgently. Tired and sleepy though she was, Frances had assumed command over the question. How like her father she was. 'We shall name him William, then,' he agreed.

He saw her smile contentedly. She would sleep now. And so he left her, with little William, his son, already slumbering in the crook of her arm.

Her premonition concerning the naming of William had all the promise of coming to pass as 1659 drew to its close.

With all his titles stripped from him by the present Rump Parliament, Richard's six months of immunity from arrest was at an end. Frances learned that he had furtively left Hampton Court and had gone into hiding. But his presence was still being felt, setting those who saw fewer problems for themselves under him than under the monarch hovering across the Channel against those who saw no hope for the country if the weak Richard were to regain his Protectorship.

'It will come to civil war again,' said Mary fearfully. 'Parliament and the Army are at each other's throats and nothing can be done about it.'

But there were those prepared to do something about it. Visualising anarchy in a land once again divided, General George Monck – until now loyal to the late Lord Protector's son, for all his weak will – gave up wrestling with his conscience. His cautious mind at last cleared of doubt, he marched south from Scotland, declaring his intention to call a free parliament, first having secretly sent an emissary to Charles Stuart to advise that he quit Spanish Flanders and hold himself ready at Breda in Holland to embark for England at the given moment. As he had anticipated, rather than his army being obstructed, it was hailed as the only body capable of restoring order.

At Hursley, Frances stood in the oak-beamed hall of Richard's home. With her was John, her brother Henry, her sister-in-law Elizabeth and her mother, Mary having chosen to stay away.

Mary had given no excuse for not attending, but Frances knew she had no real love for Richard. What small affection she had once had was entirely dissipated in contempt for his weakness in having given up.

Frances could not share her sister's sentiments. Dick had been betrayed by those who'd called themselves his friends. He was a man of too gentle a nature to rule, and that wasn't his fault. She saw it more as the fault of her father, who'd been well aware of his son's character yet had thrust a hard, exacting, dangerous office upon him. Henry would have been a far better choice, being a man who drew the affection of others, instinctively able to outwit his enemies just as his father had done. It was a mystery why her father hadn't named him, unless the two were so alike that even in death he was jealous of Henry's capabilities to reign as well as he had done. She knew all about jealousy in fathers. Hadn't she too been at the rope's end of it at one time?

Now Richard was saying goodbye to them all. He had already hugged Frances to him, tears flowing unchecked down his narrow, haggard cheeks. She'd handed little William to John so she could receive her brother's embrace. She had then taken the child back and, loath to hand him over to a nurse, stood helpless to one side while Richard took his leave of his mother and then his wife.

Dorothy's grief was heartbreaking to watch. 'Send for me, my dearest,' she wept as finally he pulled gently away from her. 'I shall wait for you, Richard, to send for me and the children. I shall wait.'

With Dorothy consigned to the arms of her mother, her father patted her shoulder ineffectually before going forward to shake his son-in-law's hand.

Farewells at an end, Frances, with her tear-damp handkerchief to her lips, watched her brother make his way into the yard where horses stood ready to take him and a manservant to the coast and then to France.

As one, the small assembly followed, prolonging that moment when he must go from their sight. In the yard, they stood in a ragged semicircle while, prior to mounting, Richard gave Henry – the brother he had so seldom seen – a last lingering gaze. But their parting handshake dissolved quickly and convulsively into a poignant embrace.

'You'd have done a better job than I,' came Richard's muffled, grief-coarsened voice.

'Who but God can say,' returned Henry, his own voice muffled.

The brothers broke apart, Dick placing his foot in the stirrup and swinging up into the saddle in one easy movement to sit looking down at his family. 'I shall return as soon as it is safe for me to do so,' he said after a moment, his voice still husky with the pain of leaving them all.

With that, like someone cutting a thread, he swung his

mount's head away from them and set off at a gallop, his manservant close behind, their horses' hooves clattering sparks off the cobbled yard.

I shall return, he had said, but as she waved with the others at his rapidly diminishing figure, Frances felt in her heart, which seemed near to breaking, that it would be many a long year before any of them would see him again.

Mary was like a young child excited by the splendour of pageantry. But for the moment her excitement held a tinge of anxiety for her sister.

'Oh, Frankie, do come. You must be with us to watch him. You're still hardly dressed for the streets, and they are already crowded. By the time we arrive we will not be able to see him at all.'

Sitting in the drawing room at Fauconberg House, Frances shook her head, ignoring the cloak her sister held out to her. 'I've no wish to see him, splendid though they say he is.'

'But you must! It has been arranged for us all to be there. You cannot be the only one who is absent, especially as you were once nearly affianced to him.'

'Nonsense!' spat Frances. 'It was nothing but a silly rumour.'

'I'm not so sure.'

'I've no wish to speak of it, nor be reminded,' huffed Frances, remaining firmly in her chair.

John gave Thomas Fauconberg an amused grin, then came to where Frances sat tight-lipped, hands clasped even tighter in her lap, determined not to go running with them all to this apparently marvellous spectacle of a king coming to reclaim his throne.

'Your sister urges you rightly, my dear,' John said quietly. 'You should be with us.'

'I shall remain here,' she returned adamantly.

It was the thirtieth birthday of King Charles II, as he was now being proclaimed. It was the twenty-ninth of May 1660, a gloriously sunny Tuesday morning. They had all listened to accounts of preparation in every town that the royal procession was due to pass through in its triumphant journey from Dover. Canterbury and Rochester were said to be ablaze with decoration and flags, the King's likeness everywhere displayed.

He had now reached London at last, and within an hour would be moving up the Strand to Whitehall.

Whitehall – Frances felt her heart grow bitter with once happy memories of her and Mary careering through its corridors and rooms, taking delight in its magnificence and their father's grandeur, and of how later she would steal furtively across its wintry gardens into the arms of Jeremiah White. Mostly she remembered the feeling of possession that she thought would never end. Now it all belonged to the King, and the whole land was rejoicing, forgetting that once upon a time they had lauded a Cromwell who'd ruled with marvellous capability over them, keeping their lives ordered and England's greatness certain.

This king – this debauched, unmarried king over whose sensual, darkly handsome looks women swooned, and who by all account made the most of each of them – could he match her father in keeping England great? She very much doubted it, on hearing the accounts of him.

'I am not,' John finally stated as Frances remained firmly in her chair, 'going to greet His Majesty with you not at my side, Frances.'

The argument had gone on half the morning, with Mary at her wit's end, alternately sulking and getting into a fume, thinking the viewing would be cancelled because of her sister's behaviour. It was a conspiracy, of course.

'How can I go if you refuse to go?' Mary cut across John's urging. 'My Tom can hardly go without me either.'

It was a conspiracy. Frances could only relent before her husband's nod of endorsement. She allowed herself a petulant sigh.

'It seems I have no choice.' She'd known all along that she'd have had none if John grew heavy-handed, though he'd never been a man for such actions.

Getting up reluctantly, she allowed her cloak to be handed to her, and without saying another word followed the others out to board Fauconberg's carriage.

London was clogged solid by the thousands who had come to see the royal entry into the City. The tightly packed crowds gave way begrudgingly before the Fauconbergs' carriage, as they had for all other carriages. But the royal route, when they reached it, was crammed even tighter. Not only were the pavements and roads crammed, but men were up on low roofs clinging to chimneys, standing on fences and on gates, and women were leaning from every window.

As they eased their way through slowly, Frances thought of other times – the days of her father's triumphant entries into the City. There had been crowds then, but never flocking from all parts of the surrounding countryside as they were now doing – maybe even from all parts of the country, by the looks of their numbers.

Never had she seen such displays of excitement.

There were tapestries and flowers everywhere; bells rang and trumpets blared; music surrounded them, the noise deafening; even the fountains were gushing wine. The cost of it all had to be beyond reckoning. To think Parliament had been so niggardly with their few petty thousands for Richard, it sickened her.

Mary, her mind far from her poor brother, was beside herself with excitement, and nearly fell from the open-sided carriage as she leapt up to see the first of two thousand horse and foot swing into view. Her husband only just managed to catch hold of her to prevent her going down into the milling crowd around them.

Frances stayed firmly in her seat. Now that the carriage had managed to get near enough to the route, she would see well enough over everyone's head. Not that she wished to look – her thoughts were on Dick, now in exile, destined to wander in foreign lands unknown and unsung. How she detested this day.

She sat with her head bowed, not caring that John was laughing at her silly attitude. All around, men and women in their best and most frivolous clothes were leaping up and down in a frenzy to see better, men with children on their shoulders, women pushing and struggling for better positions.

No one apparently recognised those in the carriage around which they surged – the two youngest daughters of the late Lord Protector. But to Frances it didn't matter. She had her own triumph, here inside her – her second child, her future, her history to echo down the ages. Her children would be able to declare that their grandfather had been a Cromwell, Oliver Cromwell, the one-time Lord Protector of this great nation. She prayed to God it would be so. She would see to it that they would reap admiration and be proud of their illustrious forebear.

It was that thought that made her heart grow unexpectedly lighter, and, perhaps caught up in the general madness as the King's approach grew nigh, she clambered to her feet without thinking. She felt John clutch at her, concerned that she in her condition might cause harm to herself. But he too was eager to see, for his father would be among the noblemen in the procession, every one clad in cloth of gold.

'Oh, look!' shrieked Mary, suddenly pointing excitedly. 'The King! Charles Stuart! Do you see him?'

A rough-looking Londoner just below her, catching her over-familiar use of the name, glared indignantly up at her.

''Ave some respect, m'lady,' he yelled above the din. 'Y'may be of some fine family but it don't give y'leave to go calling 'Is Majesty so familiar!'

Mary glanced at Frances and gave a little giggle. 'Were he to know that one of us was nearly His Majesty's wife! You'd now be queen of England!'

Frances wasn't listening. She had eyes only for the King as he came towards them, riding a snow-white charger, proudly caparisoned. He cut a splendid figure. His black breeches were swathed in gold lace, his cloak made of cloth of gold, his tall hat befeathered. His hair, curling to his shoulders, was jet black. His heavy, handsome face was swarthy, betraying the Italian blood of his mother, and above the full, sensuous lips his fine moustache was also dark. Seeing him – the man whose name had once, so briefly, been coupled with hers –

178

Frances felt her heart give a strange disconcerting leap. Yes, to think she could have been his wife . . .

He had come level with her carriage, and she caught her breath as he paused, having seen her above the heads of his subjects. His dark eyes met hers, and she saw the heavy lips part in a knowing smile, yet one that conveyed friendliness rather than contempt or ridicule. Then he offered her a slight bow. Automatically she found herself returning the courtesy, and as if a score had been amicably settled between them, he moved on, sitting tall on his horse, his head now to the front.

He knows who I am. The thought raced through her, leaving her face burning, her heart pounding, while all around the crowd roared its adoring approval of a king's gallant gesture to a woman standing up in her carriage. Some even looked up in envy, even the rough one who'd admonished Mary, but their faces held no recognition of her.

John was standing up too, his arm around her shoulder. He drew her close, his voice in her ear.

'It is a new era, my dear. We must let the past die, as it should, and be buried, as with any who die. There is no forgetting it, but we must look forward. You and I will go forward into this new age, don't you agree, my dear?'

He knew. He must have heard the rumours at that time. She nodded, watching the diminishing figure of the King sitting above the cheering crowds as he rode on his way to Whitehall. He had gone past her, as much in her life had gone past her. But as John had said, memories – precious though they were – couldn't be constant companions, nor should they be. They had to be put aside and not wept over.

The wisdom of those words suddenly hit her. She shared her life with John now. She would want for nothing, so long as she did not yearn for the past. Her husband, one day to be the third baronet Russell, loved her dearly, and she loved him equally dearly. What would she want with a king? With that thought – one that almost made her laugh out loud – suddenly the past did not matter any more.

Frances felt her spirits rise like some physical thing. She had given John a son, and now she was carrying his second child, and there would be many more, in the manner of the proliferous Russell family.

The future was here in her womb, and she very ready for that future.

Afterword

Although Charles II was a clement man, Parliament continued to wage a vendetta on his father's murderers, executing some and imprisoning others.

Nor did those already dead escape. The body of the Lord Protector Oliver Cromwell and that of Bridget's first husband Henry Ireton were exhumed and ritually beheaded, their heads spiked on poles at Westminster Hall, their headless bodies flung into a common pit at the foot of Tyburn Gallows (where Marble Arch now stands). Mary was said to have bribed the soldiers to let her take her father's body for proper burial, though where that grave lies is uncertain.

An exchange of words between Mary Fauconberg and a nobleman walking with the King some time later shows the spirit of the Cromwell women. To the King's embarrassment, the man, attempting to be witty, taunted her: 'Madam, I saw your father yesterday.'

'What then, sir?' she returned.

'He stank most abominable,' he replied.

But she remarked calmly, 'I suppose he was dead then.' When the man swore that he was, she continued. 'I thought so, else I believe he would have made you stink worse.'

Mary never had children, Jeremiah White's prediction coming true. After the death of her husband Lord Fauconberg, she remained a widow until her death in 1712 at the age of seventy-five. She openly professed her attachment to the Church of England and considered it a most perfect religion. She attended royal court, and in her old age was regarded as a curious piece of antiquity, being fresh and cheerful for all her being a great age.

Her mother, the Protectoress, survived Cromwell by only seven years, dying at Norborough, the home of her son-in-law John Claypole, and was buried in the chancery of the local church, although no memorial has been found to her memory. The treasure she hid away on her husband's death was discovered and confiscated at the Restoration, but the King, being ever courteous to women, would not let her be molested and allowed her to live out her life in modest comfort. John Claypole, Betty's husband, eventually remarried.

Of Bridget little is known. She died in 1681 at Stoke Newington, the seat of the ancient family of Fleetwood, and was buried there. It is not certain whether she had children by Fleetwood, but through her daughters by Ireton many descendants are to be found.

Dorothy Cromwell never saw her husband Richard again. She died at Hursley on the fifth of January 1675, fifteen years after he left England.

Richard Cromwell, after roaming Europe under assumed names, finally returned to England in 1680, taking the name of Clark, to live out his life at Cheshunt in contented retirement, keeping his whereabouts from even his own family. A small, somewhat poignant anecdote is handed down to the effect that, curiosity leading him to visit the House of Lords, a stranger asked him if he'd ever seen anything like it before, to which Richard replied, 'Never since I sat in that chair,' and pointed to the throne. He enjoyed a good state of health and lived to be eighty-six, dying in 1712, the same year as Mary.

Jeremiah White lived for fifty years with the wife he had been forced to marry – Frances Cromwell's lady-in-waiting. When in her old age his wife was asked about his affair with the Protector's daughter, she is recorded to have replied, 'There was something in it.'

Of Frances as wife and eventual widow of Sir John Russell, very little is known. Yet a peculiar circumstance is recorded to have arisen in regard to her giving money to an unnamed monarch while she, having married into the vastly wealthy Russell family, managed to reduce its wealth almost to nothing.

As for her children, her first son, Sir William Russell, with more patriotism than prudence, helped finish the ruin of the family fortune in trying to promote revolution – a member of the convention parliament, he wanted the throne vacant again. Finally forced to part with the estates at Chippenham, he died in 1707, dispossessed of every last acre.

Through Frances' daughter Elizabeth, however, the blood of Oliver Cromwell was introduced into the Worsley family, whose descendant is HRH the Duchess of Kent and in whose veins, ironically, also flows the blood of Charles I, whose death warrant Oliver Cromwell took part in signing.